THE GREAT OCEANS WITHIN US

KILLADA SATYANARAYANA, IPS

PRABHAT PRAKASHAN

Published by

PRABHAT PRAKASHAN PVT. LTD.
4/19 Asaf Ali Road,
New Delhi-110002 (INDIA)
e-mail: prabhatbooks@gmail.com

ISBN 978-93-5562-720-9

THE GREAT OCEANS WITHIN US
by Killada Satyanarayana, IPS

Translated by Sandeepa Guntreddy

Edition
First, 2024

Price
₹ 350 (Rupees Three Hundred Fifty Only)

Printed at
SS Japan Arts, Delhi

Foreword

Shadows and Lights

'There are great works everybody can do on this Earth.'

I don't remember where and when I read the above adage.

Yet, it stands foremost of all the sayings close to my heart.

This adage has the power to instil confidence in anyone to take up work enthusiastically.

I sometimes feel that this saying alone is enough to make lives meaningful.

Then again, I wonder why this world has so many quotations, motivators and self-help books? Why?

Why because —

Each person has a unique psychological structure.

And the internal path into each person is unique.

The light which illuminates each life comes from a different direction.

Most importantly - the internal doors to a human being can't be opened by one individual alone.

That is why... There are as many books as there are brains. There are as many sun rays as there are dark rooms.

Life is easier for one who understands it. Complicated otherwise. And, the ones who understand this secret can't just keep quiet.

> For fools who can't estimate the basic math of how much earning is enough for their own family —
>
> For the educational system that makes students learn by turbulence and by falling and getting up than through learning joyfully—
>
> For those who feel sad that a 'rose plant has thorns' rather than being happy that a 'thorn plant has roses' —
>
> For humanity that is losing its precious moments in the game played by their delusional minds —

... they strive to share their views.

Such conflagration and concern are there in my friend and author, Mr Satyanarayana, who accepts the ebbs and flows that life offers with equanimity. The outcome of that concern is this book 'The Great Oceans Within Us'.

This is not the book that extracts and compiles content from other personality development books. With his deep interest in self-consciousness, the author goes to the depths of a man controlled by his mind since times immemorial. He attempts to explain this simple yet profound mystery through the complementariness of shadows and lights in one's life.

He beautifully correlates the ocean with mankind. Although at the surface of the ocean, we find turbulences like tides, waves, and cyclones, we find quietness as we go deep. In addition, we find precious stones, gems and invaluable treasures as we go deeper. Likewise, at the surface of our lives, we face many dilemmas, dualities, pleasures and pains. However, once we go deeper, we will find immense joy, peace and oneness among all. So, he rationally convinces that mankind should search for solutions to one's problems by going deep inside oneself than getting perturbed by external situations.

As a result, this book showcases that an individual can search and find real gems at the depths of his inner world.

Since the author of this book is also a poet, it appears that the Moon is shining on these oceans.

'There are great works everybody can do on this Earth.'

Even recognising, with awareness, that I have such great oceans within me is also the greatest achievement by itself.

Best Wishes

Bhagavantham
A well-known writer in Telugu
Kotthagudem, AW

Author's Note

Everyone was baffled when a 17-year young girl committed suicide. She left to a world where there is no place to fulfil her dreams.

'What difficult responsibilities has she shouldered to take this decision?' said one.' What life has she seen to come to this conclusion?', another said. 'Is failure in academic exams a solid reason to take one's life?' questioned everyone.

Who knows what's going on in her mind? Who knows what dreams she has built around the exam results and how the failure collapsed the society's expectations around her! Can we say that we need a great reason like the Tsunami or an earthquake to die? Or should we say something as rational as a war a solid basis to a soldier to die?

A war is to a soldier as an exam is to a student. That's what we have made it look like. But whether it is a student or a soldier, doesn't everyone have a right to live? Children are studying as if they are gearing up for a war. Is the entire ecosystem of education a platform for a moneymaking warfront? Is learning not a joyful process anymore?

Why are life skills not taught in our schools?' asked my friend.

'Even if we simply allowed them to live, that's more than enough,' said I.

This is how we all live, so horrendously - by pushing, stamping, crossing and pulling each other. We are greedy. We are weak. There is either fear or sorrow in any direction we see. Is life supposed to be such a gruelling punishment, or are we insanely abusing it? What if someone didn't become a doctor? What if they didn't conquer the peak? What if they chose to take a less trodden path? Can't we live the way we are? Whether a painter, a player, a musician, aren't we all human? Isn't that a worthy life?

Let iron be like iron; let gold be like gold without comparing them. Don't we need both? Don't both have unique qualities, and have they not flowered from the same mother Earth just like we all did? How is one superior over the other? Who defines these metrics? Are these definitions making any sense?

No ant thinks that a human is great. To an ant, its life is everything. So does an earthworm or a mosquito. Who defines who is more worthy of living on this planet? Remember, it is not that we alone have expectations from life; even life has expectations. There are always tasks allotted to each of us based on our nature. When they find us, life takes its natural course because we have the required capability to execute them. Through them only, we find fulfilment and satisfaction and life blossoms. That's what life is expecting from us, to let it live its natural course.

Why? Why have you not questioned these aspects every time you compared and let yourself down and others down?

To rain, clouds are a must. Similarly, to live, we need day and night. Let there be good and bad. Let there be joy and sorrow. Let there be beings of all varieties. Are these all not shining through the rays of the same Sun? Does the Sun disfavour anything? Does the Earth disfavour anything? So, who are we to discriminate and disfavour? Are we not conditioned to choose one over the other ignorantly? On the contrary, we are prepared to choose one and reject another. Is this even feasible in the science of Creation?

Creation is all about complementariness. Day & night, joy & sorrow, success & failure, feminine & masculine, yes & no, reward & punishment... How can we foolishly long for just one without its twin? If you observe, life is an exciting game and a beautiful song and should be just lived. So why can't we play it joyfully, singing along to its beautiful song, experiencing everything in its way? Why complicate it for no good and then propound theories to solve it? What a criminal waste of valuable life energies! Don't you think so?

Come. Let us accept life with both hands with all its differences, turbulences, and complementariness. Come, let us live it like a festival spreading its happiness. Before you read any further, I have a confession to make. I haven't followed everything I said here in this book. Yet, I did follow some and succeeded. Failed following some. Trying to follow some consciously despite resistance. So, please read this book without any 'ifs' and 'buts'. I am as imperfect as you are in my way. Yet, I want to see things the way they are without applying my one-sided logical lens. In this endeavour, if I can help you move forward by one step... it takes me one more step forward.

Killada Satyanarayana

Translator's Note

'If somebody offers you an amazing OPPORTUNITY, but you are not sure you can do it, SAY YES, then learn how to do it!'

The above quote indeed summarises my whole experience with the English translation of Mr Killada Satyanarayana's Telugu book 'Manishi Lopali Maha Samudralu'. When I started reading his works, I felt I was talking to myself and experienced an outburst of my internal turbulences with life's experiences. Without my knowledge, I internalised the content and readily expressed my interest in lending voice to his content for my YouTube podcasts. And when I asked the author if he ever thought of getting this book translated into English to reach a broader audience, that's when he said. Why don't you do it in English?' So I grabbed the opportunity and thus began my journey with translation.

As I indirectly mentioned at the beginning, I was initially intimidated due to many reasons. Firstly, it is impossible to match the beauty of the original writing. Secondly, I didn't wish to disappoint the author, who had already created a significant impact with the depth of his experiences and impressive writing. Thirdly, being convent educated, I am not too well-versed with the essence and profoundness of the Telugu language, even though I speak the same every day. Yet, I wanted to answer in the affirmative because I genuinely admired his works and wanted to be associated with his writings.

The book grapples honestly with thought-provoking current trends of humanity that are universal and makes some acceptable propositions that can lead to new thought processes for the readers. In addition, the author's skill in using commonly used words and real-life examples makes it very relatable and easy to follow. As much as I learned from his writings, I had to unlearn many habitual lines of thinking to imbibe new methods for joyful experiences in the future.

I thank the author, **Mr Killada Satyanarayana,** for giving me this golden opportunity for his venture with an amateur like me. His impeccable support, diligent reviews, and constructive feedback throughout the process was the motivation I needed to complete the work that I so enthusiastically started. In this process, I felt as if I was pursuing a doctorate in the philosophy of life. Like a faithful public servant and a police officer, Mr Satyanarayana taught me the ways of discipline, the importance of relentless hard work, and the rule of wholehearted commitment to succeed in any unchartered territory.

While translating is one big part of the whole game, reviewing it is equally daunting, subtle, and continuous. Many well-wishers and experts played a significant role in the review process. Foremost, I'm grateful to my friend, **Ms Manjari Mandava.** She is a fine mix of talent who has a bird's eye view of the overall delivery. Her sincere effort in improvising the delivery is invaluable.

I am grateful to my good omen, **Ms Rekha Madiraju** for proofreading my work. She has always made time for what's important to me and I count that as an immense blessing.

I thank my well-wisher, **Ms Nisha Jagadesh,** for verifying the definiteness of the content. Her vast exposure to Indian books of knowledge and extensive global travel experience truly brought a new zest to this book. I thank **Ms Aditi Kapur** an information art and design student, for inspiring me with her illustrative designs and artwork. I feel blessed to have worked with expert designers like **Ms Shweta Nair,** who always provided critical reviews of my work. I owe my entire family and many invisible hands for their ongoing support. Finally, I am grateful to my spouse, **Kirankumar Arnepalli,** for his immense faith, regard and support for whatever I pursue. The world is a beautiful place because of all of them.

I wish and pray that my English translation succeeds in propagating Mr Satyanarayana's devoted enthusiasm towards the inner journey humanity must traverse. I am happy to be a small part of this book's journey that has the universal appeal to cater to audiences of all ages across the seven oceans.

Although I could not match the original in its intensity, grip, flow, or beauty, I must say that I put in my best efforts and gave it my all. Any limitation you find in my translation has to do with my capability as a writer and should not be construed as a parameter to assess the eminence of the original content (written in Telugu, 'మనిషి లోపలి మహా సముద్రాలు').

Sandeepa Guntreddy

Acknowledgements

Nothing can be built without support. The same is the case with this book. Before culminating into a complete book, every essay in this book was published independently in different Telugu magazines. So, I extend my warm gratitude to the editors of 'Chinuku' and 'Missimi' Telugu monthly magazines.

Whatever I have expressed here isn't an excerpt lifted out of a book. I have been in varying degrees of a dilemma as I evolved with every passing day. These dilemmas shaped my personality and have shown me the way ahead. Indeed, all these essays stemmed from personal difficulties and dilemmas. How can I wade through these Great Oceans without the support of my family and friends — parents, sister, wife, children, friends, and teachers. I owe them a lot.

I also thank my friends and writers, Mr Harsha Vardhan and Mr Bhagavantam, for their encouragement. Of course, one cannot miss appreciating Mr Bhagavantam's foreword for this book.

I extend my sincere gratitude to the most revered Dr N. Gopi, Sahitya Academy Awardee, for his blessings.

Above all, I am grateful for **Ms Sandeepa's** perseverance to bring this book to English language readers. She felt that this book would shape the lives of millions of youth adults. Without the English translation, this goal could not be achieved. I am thankful for her contribution. After reading her book 'The Bhagavad Gita for College Students', which is well-received in various cities and colleges, I thought she was the right person to be trusted with the translation of my work.

Thank you all for your contributions to my journey.

'Life is the Gift of the Nature
Beautiful Life is the Gift of Wisdom'

- A Greek Adage

-**KillAda Satyanarayana, IPS**

Contents

Luck and Destiny

Luck and destiny can be mapped to Cod and Ghost, respectively. If you ask anyone if these exist, the answer is, as you know — two ways. We choose the former if we succeed and pick the latter otherwise.

There happened to be two students — one is good at studies, and another at games. Over time, both of them prospered in their respective fields. But, on the other hand, some of their laid-back classmates didn't show much progress in their lives. They neither do anything significant nor show interest in taking up something. So, they grouped with like-minded folks and passed the time. All the while, they make statements, 'They have just got lucky', about their classmates who succeeded.

Looking at her drunkard and wayward husband, a wife grumbles how destiny played with her life. While some work smart and lead a comfortable life, others succumb to bad habits and lose their wealth. We often see that the one born in slums thinks that the wealthy lot is lucky. We also hear of people who die in accidents and natural calamities. Without second thoughts, this is what many tend to say about the survivors,

'Thank God, how lucky that they survived!'. But, on the other hand, we speak about those who don't make it, 'Who can change their fate if they are destined to die this way!'.

Let me ask you one thing very clearly. Are there lucky people in this world? If they do, how many are these? If this is tricky to answer, try this. How many unlucky fellows are there, and who are they?

We haven't stopped categorizing as poor, rich, old, and ill to date. We are even unconsciously classifying people as happy and unhappy lots. Why can't we eradicate bad luck in a world where we have succeeded in eliminating deadly diseases like Polio, Smallpox, and Yaws?

Could you think about this? Do you believe the cuckoo that sings well is luckier than the crow that caws? Also, have you ever thought if the King of the jungle, the Lion, is more fortunate than the deer?

Even a blade of grass is as beautiful as a rose when seen without bias. There is nothing like more or less when it comes to relishing beauty.

Didn't you ever hear people grieving about Africa and how Cod has been so cruel to them that they must face so many hardships? Yet, is Africa not rich in natural resources? If so, where is the problem? Isn't it a case of lack of human endeavour? For a minute, let us change our direction towards the Middle East; don't they have everything they need except that their hearts are raging war fields. That is why I think poverty is not despicable; poverty of the spirit is.

Are earthquakes, cyclones, and diseases, symbols of bad luck? A lorry hit a small boy who was sleeping on the roadside. A diligent student failed in his exams. A hardworking farmer lost his crop. An innocent girl got molested by lustful eyes. We hear of all such incidents around us. Don't we? Think about our first reaction to all these realities. 'What a fate!' 'I wish Cod could show some mercy?'

Let us ask ourselves if these occur due to the lack of Cod's mercy or our errors?

How do we judge luck?

Based on birth? On their success? Or on escape from mishaps?

Two people should not be assessed differently if the only differences are due to factors beyond their control. However, we judge others based on their origin, caste, religion, race, region etc., which are not in their control. Therefore, they resort to luck and destiny.

All over the world, people clamour for justice.

But, does justice exist in its true spirit? The distribution of resources is not based on an egalitarian principle. Some are favoured profusely. And some are poorly ignored. This imbalance has happened overtime for various reasons.

Where justice is left to the mercy of the distributor, then it shelters in caves of destiny. Who is responsible for this? Who is facing its brunt?

Again, the time we live in is not in our control. Living in the Nazi period, the Taliban's rule or pandemic times is not in our hands. If they got shifted elsewhere, the affected people would have led exemplary lives.

Some are born healthy, some with genetic deformation. Sometimes these genetic disorders occur due to manmade holocausts like nuclear explosions and the usage of toxic chemicals. Some become victims of these reasons beyond our control.

The constitution of our body is also not in our control.

If we count on the things beyond our control, our Will to act will be affected adversely. Then our actions or mind will not be free. This means they function under fear.

So, how do we respond to such situations?

- Deny them completely

- First accept, then ignore and move on
- Live with it while struggling.

Which one would you adopt?

Both luck and destiny are born out of results. Getting more than expected is luck, and less is destiny. Does anyone begin his life with the presumption of luck? Or destiny? We judge destiny based on profit and loss. As a matter of fact, this is the hard reality.

The result is like a mirror. It reflects the actual image. But are we ready to face the truth?

Some say that marriages are made in Heaven. In that case, why are many in wedlock experiencing hell? Who is to blame? God or human? Isn't our misunderstandings and egos ruling the roost instead of living in harmony and humbleness? Come on, how can we tag all those as supernatural or beyond human understanding, which our tiny minds can't conceive? When will we own up to our mistakes? Aren't we seriously flawed in hiding in the blame game drama?

We call old age unlucky and youth lucky. How have we missed noticing that it is the same 'us' going through all these stages, from childhood to old age!

Isn't it the play of our delusive minds and our value systems that can't see and treat everything with equanimity?

Which moron starts his life journey thinking that he is lucky? And which dimwit ends his life initially, thinking that he is unlucky. For that matter, doesn't sadness touch those who get more than they desire?

Also, when a person tries repeatedly and still fails, it is not because he didn't try enough or tried the wrong way. Sometimes it is not designed to happen. Our scriptures say that today's situations are determined based on our karma from the past. In addition, today's actions decide our future. So, despite our best efforts, some things don't go as we please. Sometimes, we think our plan is good, but the divine may have a better plan that we cannot see right now. So, we may not be a failure, but the loss may instead be a path for something better. Thus, it is essential to stay optimistic and not compromise on our efforts.

To change destiny (which is nothing but karma), all that we should do is correct our actions and follow our dharma — not lie, not hurt others in any way, fulfil our duties without expecting results, not compare with others, not let jealousy or anger come in our way. And if things still do not go the way we want them to, it is because there is something better in-store, or we are just letting karma play its role. Remember, the result of an action is not in our hands and should not be our worry. Only our effort matters, and we should accept any outcome.

Therefore, let us understand that luck and destiny are consequences of our doings. If things went as desired, we called it luck. Otherwise, we tagged it as destiny.

We have both 'passionate and hardworking' employees and 'unmotivated and lazy' ones in the workforce. While the former group works towards the results, the latter survives on the fruit of others' labour. Yet, they don't stop glaring at those who flourish and indulge in passing statements such as 'Timing is everything you know. My right time is yet to come. Therefore,

I have to stay patient.' This is how they end up spending life listlessly looking for the right time.

Good times and bad times are like day and night. Both of them are part of the day. Hence, wishing for the day without the night will only make the whole day dark because of our skewed expectations.

There is something unique about each of us. That is where our strength lies. We need to spare time to identify in which field this is. Otherwise, we will do things that don't fit us and fall for supernatural powers and superstitions to come to our rescue.

So, you tell me, how can someone who is brilliant at dance and enjoys it thoroughly be expected to be happy and prosperous in an accounting job?

On the other hand, how can someone excellent at sciences be thrown into the sports field and expected to make it to podium finish?

Remember, the probability of someone succeeding in an area that doesn't suit them is possible with hard work. However, isn't he disabled internally with no satisfaction and joy in what he does? That's the whole point - to be happy.

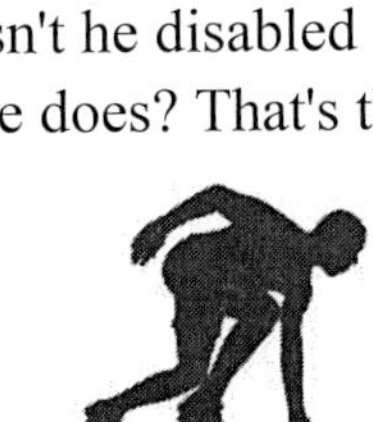

Success is like winning a lottery. If you chase it, you will miss the joy of winning your heart. Happiness comes with heartfelt work.

No one gets lucky just winning in a lottery draw. It is not always true that the one who wins is competent. If these people are termed lucky, they shouldn't lose and should be part of the

Fortune 500 list by now. However, we see some of these even going bankrupt.

So, do you still think that there are lucky ones?

When we see others wealth and fame, it seems that way. Right? When we look at someone's successes, we whine, 'Everything they lay their hands on turns into gold. How lucky!'

When we hear of rags to riches stories and the unimaginable celebrity status of ordinary people, we say it is all because of their luck. Yet, we don't dare to see and digest their values, experiences, learnings, and persistent efforts to get there.

So, what do you think their secrets are?

- Acceptance of what is inevitable and being grateful for what is available
- A Identifying opportunities or having the insight to create one
- Listening to one's conscience before taking decisions
- Following diligently with optimism once the decision is m made with clarity
- A Ability to steer through life skilfully
- Resilient attitude to convert mishaps into good fortunes

Isn't the famous quote 'Luck is what happens when preparation meets opportunity' so true?

Of course, one needs to buy a ticket to win the lottery (Luck). Still, more importantly, one needs to put themselves in a position (Preparation) to buy the ticket and pursue Luck. In this preparation, intuition is the key. Just as the birds and animals find their prey on their lookout, even we come across suitable opportunities. We need the right mindset to identify and utilize the ones that match our inclinations and conscience.

All those people whom you call lucky have a relaxed demeanour. Their general attitude is to be open to chances. Instead of just daydreaming about their wish list, they focus on doing well with what is right in their hands. Some throw parties to acquire friends and mourn as if they got trapped amongst opportunists. For some, friends come looking for them and find happiness in their success. Even in this kind of an occurrence, people don't stop venting, 'One should be lucky to get such good friends, you know.' But unfortunately, they don't understand that Luck depends on how we look at life.

What is bad luck? Putting down the effort under the carpet. Succumbing to unfavourable conditions. Real luck happens when you rise above the situation, learn and move on.

If you want to wait until all problems and limitations go away to start something, you must wait until you approach your grave. You don't have to superimpose others' lives onto yourself and dramatize mishaps for yourself.

What imaginings are these that haven't happened to you? Yet, you chose to live in fear. I ask you. What do you call a person who fears something that doesn't exist?' What life quality do you think these people experience when they have only complaints of the past, doubts about the future and indifference to the present?

Let us understand that both destiny and luck are related to the past.

When there is a gap between expected and experienced and move in different directions, we call it 'destiny or fate'. On the other hand, when the expected and experienced meet at a point and go hand in hand, we call it 'luck or fortune'.

Both 'fate' and 'fortune' are dependent on faith. Man, always believes that there is something beyond his experiences. He guesses that there is a force behind the universe, which is not comprehendible to one's logic but has the power to decide one's success or defeat. It is these forces referred to as 'Divine or Destiny[1].

Man is always curious to know about these forces, have control over them and make them work in his favour. For this, he takes refuge in rituals, yagnas, and sacrifices. Becomes anxious to know his future. Follows a horoscope or astrology. And gets lost in choosing such paths.

Sheer commitment and relentless efforts make men. Faith in oneself brings them close to home. There's no shortcut to Adam's fruit. No excuses will save you from hell. You alone got to swim.

Trust in external forces is like studying in the lightning. Likewise, trust in one's internal energies is like learning in the sunlight.

Some people abdicate worldly life. They suppress their desires. They claim that they obtained divine powers. Some of them claim to be demigods too. For others, they are divinely blessed. In common parlance, divine grace is also luck. Some surrender before Cod during difficulties. And some approach an astrologer for a bright future. These are the people whom you see wearing stones and gems. They follow days and timings. In both these cases, man believes in external support, as you see.

Man tries to find answers for all his queries from his previous births. People justify their destiny or luck in that light of karma. Since they can't change past actions, they adjust to the present.

We can understand our behaviour, observe our thoughts, and change our actions, to make our lives lively and cross our troubles with ease by being aware and being present.

The future is the projection of the present. The present is in the hands of presence. Hence, be present. We may not know our future. But we can study our present life.

Finding excuses for our failures is like looking for horns on deer. But unfortunately, relying on excuses or reasons and finding horns on deer are equally dangerous. Instead, one should believe in their energies and work intensely for a cause with sheer commitment.

Most of us don't want to take responsibility for our actions. Instead, we depend on others for the decisions and their consequences. As a result, we prefer remaining idol followers. Why? Because we always fear the consequences of our decisions.

How justifiable is it to delegate the responsibility of our life to others? Isn't it like asking someone to take medicine for your ailments or sitting behind the driver's seat?

Trust, you are the master of your life.

Comparison and Competition are Like Racehorses.

They Entice First, Enslave Next. Beware.

Yet, let us not fall into the trap of ego. Doing things mindlessly will land us in trouble. One should not be self-centred with success. The ego will not only ruin us but also everyone around us. Doesn't it?

Our actions should answer questions of'why' and 'how'. Our actions should match with our nature and our way of life. We should not build our life based on others' opinions. We should not lead our lives in comparison or competition with others. Our way of living should take root in our life only. To come out of the shackles of luck and destiny and to lead a happy life, there are six ways:

Accept

Accept the people and things as they or we are (Attractive or Unattractive: Intelligent or Innocent: Lean or Overweight). More importantly, accept and respect one's self to gain confidence. Beware of the traps of competition and comparison and stay away from them. They are honey traps.

Observe

Observe our thoughts, actions and feelings. This keeps us in the present state.

Observe our thoughts silently and impartially during failures or fortunes. Observe that they shouldn't take you on the wrong route. Let us embrace our actions as they open doors to solve and grow.

Practice

Practice what you preach. Practice what you think. Bridge the gap between thoughts, words and actions. Our actions firm and evolve our ideas and beliefs for betterment.

The friction in life develops when thoughts and actions travel opposite. Assess how many times our thoughts and actions travelled together and separately. Try to get them closer in the count, and this practice will guide us in our life's path.

Grateful

Be grateful for what we are and for what we have. Let us not complain in comparison. Comparison takes away the liking towards what we own. Even the dearest ones will not give us happiness with the complaining attitude. Hence, see good in all. Satisfy with things.

Let us be appreciative and thankful for what we have and use words from the heart to express our gratitude.

Clarity

Have clarity on what you want, what you need, what needs to be done and what you do. In the absence of clarity, confusion prevails. In confusion, beliefs and superstitions rule the roost. Hence, have clarity of thoughts and actions despite the complexity of the problem at hand.

Detachment

We need not run away from worldly affairs. Nor shall we be submerged by worldly things. Let us live in balance by practising detachment to the results of our efforts. To live, you have to earn. To earn, you have to learn. To learn, you have to work.

The remuneration for the work shall be like a compass. It shall not be like a knife on the neck.

Let us understand that destiny and luck are related to one's efforts, focus and sheer commitment. It's all about having faith in yourself. Let us realize that the people who made history is not a result of luck. Instead, let us recognize that they dedicated their lives to giving joy to their hearts or working for a meaningful cause.

Let us own and take responsibility for our thoughts and actions, practice them by being grateful with clarity and detachment for the results. Then, it will be a happy and fearless life.

To Those Who Believe in Their Sweat, Luck is a Myth.

To Those Who Believe in Luck,

An Effort is But a Waste of Valuable Time.

❑

Listening

I find two kinds of people as I dig deeper. One, a listener. Another, a speaker.

You might be taken aback by this statement because you think everyone speaks and listens. But, then, how about people who cannot speak and cannot hear? That is why I asked you to go deep. Even people who can't hear can listen.

We hear sound. Hearing is physical. The difference between hearing and listening is the mind. Listening is a psychological action. While hearing is associated with capacity, listening with capability. But, how attentively are we listening?

People listen as per their nature. They listen as is their situation. They listen through their experiences. In expectations, they listen in one way; in happiness, another way. In fear or distress, they listen differently.

Our sense organs work always - we can see, hear, smell, taste, and always feel- but when we are not in a calm and happy state of mind, the functions do not impact the brain.

\Ne see what happens around us, we also hear, but we do not listen, i.e,, the signals do not process well in our brain. For example, when we are sad and fearful, notice that our ears close their doors. In such a state, we don't understand whatever is being said. Where the mind is not free, the doors of change naturally close.

Children listen so freely. And that causes them to go about their life relaxed. They are neither afraid of tomorrow nor concerned about yesterday. They don't care about what others think. Unbothered by people and opinions, children are like buds about to blossom. But, unfortunately, it is us, grown-ups, that try to shape them. Like a gardener, who sizes each plant, we impose our opinions on them. We sculpt their minds to listen to what we want them to. We teach them customs and traditions. We build walls around their buds. We fill the soil with fertilizers and crops with pesticides.

The mind which is filled with the air of 'I am so and so. I want so and so' cannot listen. The same feeling creates the distance between husband and wife, officer and subordinates, and even between two countries.

To listen, one's mind should be like a farm that welcomes the rain with eager hands. Interest and attention are the two hands of listening.

Attention is important in listening. Past and future become extinct in attention. Attention comes with curiosity. In a class of forty, do all the students listen to the teacher in the same way? If you ask any question, each one gives a different answer.

I mostly meet people with petitions, manoeuvres, and boasts from where I sit. I hear people are busy talking about monetary issues. The world revolves around economics and materialistic things. Everyone who has it and those who don't care only for investments and returns.

My childhood softly nudges me as I vent out my dissatisfaction with things around me — the games we played between the trees, the mounds we created with sand at the river shore, the fun we had with dandelion flowers, and the songs we sang in the rain. It feels like even the rocks and pebbles spoke to us when I think of all these.

Recently, my friend told me that he didn't feel anything as his three-year-old child curled around his neck and murmured in his ears. He also mentioned that he couldn't listen to the stream flowing behind his house, even in complete silence. Nothing catches his attention, he complains, not even family affairs. He adds that he feels surreal. His mind seems void. Why doesn't he regard himself as faux if that is the case?

A proper spiritual practice doesn't mean avoiding sounds; it is to find convenience even amidst them.

Everyone hears the Bible, the Quran, and the Bhagavad Gita in prayers. But how many actually listen to the words of God?

"A keen listener is like flour in the hands of a baker, and words are like water added to the flour. The baker is the expert. He will use the appropriate amount of each ingredient as he deems necessary." - Rumi says.

Bats can listen to the sounds of the creatures moving underwater. But, unfortunately, a man can't even hear the cry of a fellow human reverberating through the tears. Some people don't listen, even though their job is to listen. Unfortunately, we don't pay attention, although our schedule is to listen. Leaders find people frustrating, doctors find patients irritating, teachers find students a nuisance, and police find victims disgusting. Even the one who sits under a 'May I Help You' board gets irritated when someone approaches him. There is also a misconception that the more we avoid listening to others, the more people consider us great. Another misnomer is that if someone is not giving time, they are busy. And 'busy' means they are celebrities.

If we have to listen to others carefully, first, we should open the door of our hearts. Then, we need to bring our revving thoughts that got unleashed to a standstill. But unfortunately, we often listen to what others say through our experiences and perspectives. That is why there is a practice of 'First doubt it. Then accept it.' has become prevalent in our culture.' As a result, the gap amongst us remains. Only when we receive the people, situations, other creatures, or nature as-is we can listen to them. When we listen to them, we see the beauty within.

To listen doesn't mean to ignore our voice. On the contrary, it is to light the wick of our thoughts with a candle. Ears would have been unnecessary if our thoughts were enough.

Be it children or adults, one has to ask the unknown. The feeling of knowing everything will spoil the taste of listening. Asking involves listening, the same as speaking. Modesty is vital to ask anything. To ask means to garland the other person's heart. To listen doesn't mean to hear the sounds. Listening means understanding the meaning that is not uttered by mouth. There is feeling even in the absence of sound. It has nothing to do with the lexicons or the grammar. Grasping the essence behind the words is what listening is. Listening isn't about resisting, criticizing, arguing or hindering. It's about remaining silent and just grasping.

People are ignorant of the thin line between suggestion and interference. Even a tiny tip may make some people feel their personal space is being infringed. So, to resist any suggestion, they build a bunker around them. On the other hand, some people have benefited from getting the right advice at the right time. Such a gesture works like medicine for the listener.

Listening means giving. Talking means taking. Giving means making room for others' thoughts in our hearts. Our heart expands while listening. It contracts while talking.

So, how to listen? First, Stop telling more. And eliminate distractions and focus on the context. Our thought waves don't stop even for a moment and are anxious to cross the coast. They are bloating to win over the world in comparisons and competitions with overflowing words, but thoughts are left entirely at sea. Some people talk non-stop without even taking a breath, as if the other person will grab the chance to conquer them. They think they know everything. They try their best to captivate the other person with their knowledge. They are scared that others will belittle them if they don't speak.

"The only thing I know is that I know nothing," as said by a Greek philosopher, Socrates is the only first step to listening.

Listening is not like lightning in the sky that shines and goes off instantly. It is not a hill that doesn't acknowledge good and bad. Instead, it is a free-flowing river jubilantly touching the edges of an abyss. It grows in four phases and becomes a river known as listening.

- The first phase is **attention.** It is about listening attentively with an open-mind. In this stage, one shouldn't judge the speaker or the matter. Even reading is a kind of listening.
- The second phase is **understanding.** It is essential to understand the objective and the essence of what is being said. Usually, we tend to listen with our knowledge, thoughts, experiences, and culture. Yet, unfortunately, listening is also influenced by the speaker's position, status, colour, and looks. As a result, the distance between the speaker and the listener remains the same.
- The third phase is **assimilation.** Assimilation here means to process the information as per our personal style. It allows the information to step in through our brain. Our understanding circulates among our body cells like blood.
- The fourth phase is **action.** Before we put the assimilated information into motion, we must analyze it to determine its acceptability. Once we set our incorporated information into action with heart, it transforms into our creation.

This journey called 'listening' takes us to our destination.

Speaker should practice condensing an hour of talk into fifteen minutes. Similarly, they should practice condensing a fifteen-minute speech into five minutes. Only then can a listener feel fortunate to listen to a few valuable words rather than being unfortunately bombarded with a thousand words. Moreover, he will feel more comfortable listening to ten words than having hours spent listening to hundred words.

This is when we can establish a thought bridge between a listener and a speaker. Walking on such a bridge is a joy for any listener.

Most of us are dictators. We like to listen - only if it matches our thought process and frequency. Even governments, organizations, and systems will only listen to what they like. We enjoy the entertaining parrots around us that talk only about what we want to hear or repeat our words. Anyone who talks otherwise is considered a rebel. The fate of a rebellion is rejection and suppression. In this way, we are nurturing the 'yes boss' culture.

With insightful observation, I feel that human beings are primarily biased. Some only hear for their immediate advantage. In other words, they only hear with the outcome in mind. They perceive their life to be on a straight line. To them, anything beyond and besides this straight line is dark. Anything they listen to is heard on the same frequency for those who plan each day. People of this nature prefer carbon copies of themselves. They repeatedly hear the same song so that there are no fluctuations or variations in life. They frame a schedule for a week and follow it for the rest of their lives. Or they blindly follow the path walked by many.

Some are like fossils. They live as if life is a punishment. They don't like listening to anything. Not even to themselves. They don't welcome anything. Their lives are like dilapidated buildings that aren't worth repairs or renovation. So, how can anyone make them listen to new tunes in such a state?

Some people live in utter confusion. They listen to whatever is said by anyone. They don't recognize their nature. They are not particular about doing anything or about its approach. They listen to the satisfaction of their stomach, not their mind. This is just like some people read cheap books to pass the time.

Remember, we don't have to listen to everything. Also, it's not possible either. We are not capable enough to listen to everything. However great scripture is, what's the point in listening to it without understanding? Despite our best efforts, can we keep a balloon stable in the air?

The grievance of many people is not their poverty, but that there's no one to listen to them. Individuals want to vent their feelings. The plight of those who don't get an opportunity to express themselves is beyond description. Some feel that they need to be heard. When heard, they think that they are relieved from half their pain. Of all the world's problems, most are of the heart rather than of finance. To find someone who listens to you is like finding an oasis in a desert.

Centuries rolled by with the money flown like a river for the advancement of the poor. Did it wipe their tears? How many countries haven't declared the elimination of poverty as their motto?

Yet, the nature of poverty has changed but not the form. Despite many years, the hands that ask continue to ask, and the hands that accumulate wealth continue to gather. Why? Is it because the hands that distribute don't listen to the need of the hands that take?

A famous saying implies - 'The speaking mouth looks down upon the listening ear.' So why are we looking down upon the ones who listen? The number of people who listen is few in this world. Their number is depleting day by day. When the rare is valuable, then why aren't the ears valuable?

Know that

- Only an individual who is confident in his beliefs but still willing to change for the better
- Only an individual who respects everyone's views as much as he respects his
- Only an individual who genuinely wants a solution to his problems or genuinely wants to solve other's problems
- Only an individual who truly wants to be a better person by competing with himself and not with others
- Only an individual who cares without prejudices

Can be a good listener.

And how many such individuals do we really encounter?

The individual who is in the speaking position thinks of himself as superior. It is like the man in the upper status who feels that it is his right to tell the one below him. He considers the one who listens to him as less knowledgeable or ignorant.

Some don't listen at all. To share our thoughts with such people is as complex as digging a well in the desert.

Some confine their life to some set of ideologies. Anything and everything outside these ideologies is null and void to them. They filter everything they hear through their beliefs.

If there is no difference of opinions, will there be progress in society?

So long as there is diversity, there will be differences. Diversity is the beauty of creation. The opinion is an integral part of diversity.

We need to recognize that not only tigers but deers also have opinions. Therefore, there should not be any discrimination against views. Not just the cuckoo; we need to listen to the crow as well.

We should not listen with preconceived notions. Opinions can be tools to express one's heart openly. However, they may become hindrances to listening. Everyone should have an opportunity to communicate - a King, a soldier, a husband, a wife. And there should be a heart to listen to them.

As Greek philosopher said "We have two ears and one mouth so that we can listen twice as much as we speak".

Why is there a conflict? When our opinion clashes with that of the others. For example, students listen to their teacher with their opinion. Hence friction. A husband listens to his wife's words through his ideas. When children say that they are interested in a specific subject or group in college, parents don't listen to them. Instead, they argue that it doesn't have better career prospects. In this conflict, how much energy is dissipated or wasted? In the end, what do we achieve? However, if we listen to our children and let them pursue their interests, who knows what wonders they would create. If each one listens to the other, society will become a big family.

There is pleasure in listening. There is happiness in listening freely. If we force ourselves to listen to something, there's anguish. Listening is not the problem. It's like the tree being amused by the sounds of the birds.

Without consciousness or dynamism, the plant and log are the same. The day an individual stops listening, he becomes a fossil. Sometimes I get the idea that it would have been better if there was a legal punishment for not listening.

Listen. Problems will melt away like snow. Why are many issues still burning between two countries, two religions, two faiths, and two races? Like, two people, even two countries are adamant about their opinions. They don't listen to each other. They are ready to cut down the entire tree but refuse to give a fallen fruit to the other.

Terrorism and fanaticism are growing like diseases just because of not listening. Right?

If we listen, will this land still be wet with bloodshed? Would so many wars, world wars, have taken away so many lives?

Thankfully, a few people listen, causing some level of peace. If no one had listened to anyone, this Earth would have become deaf and dumb by now. By listening only, we respect the word. By talking properly only, we give importance to listening. If the listeners can separate water from the milk like the swans, the speakers won't mix water in the milk of talking.

For the world to become one family, listening is the only means. Through listening, people of different races, religions, countries will mingle well. Doubts and superiority can be filled with listening. Pleading someone to believe you, harassing through doubting... all these sound useless to me. So why do you doubt anyone or anything? Listen to the other person with a broad heart.

Like the white includes all the seven colours, listening covers all the values. Isn't it? Just like how the stream quenches one's thirst, listening can make all problems disappear. Honey bees can sense how much nectar is there in the flowers. How does a spider make each web thread with the same thickness, density, and spacing? Who told them? However, we believe that our children will learn only if we tell them. Let us teach our children to listen through our practice of listening. Let us show them the trees that listen with the leaves as their ears. Let us allow our children to listen to the sky, the birds, the animals, the rivers, the land, the people. Let us teach them to love them all. Listening is the natural fragrance of a heart that loves.

LET ALL PEOPLE LISTEN

Sarve Jana Sravana Bhavantu

❑

Yes and No

The journey of our inner world has two streams, Yes and No. While taking a dip in the former stream cleanses us, a dip in the latter creates suffocation.

The seed to our 'Yes-No' nature is rooted in our upbringing. Frankly, our upbringing is infused with a 'No' atmosphere rather than a 'Yes'. As a result, we focus too much on what should not be done than what can be done.

'Don't eat this.' 'Don't talk like this.' 'Don't do like this.' 'Don't behave like this.'

We get our parent's acceptance only when we diligently follow their 'No' instructions. The teacher resorts to the stick to teach the child the don'ts in school. In this way, we give more importance to bending than growing.

Do you know what it takes for our brain to process a simple instruction like 'Don't Talk' vs 'Maintain Silence'? While the first one depletes energy by placing pressure on our rebellious mind, the second one assertively shows us the productive way.

For instance, in the below examples, while the first one creates stress, the second one shows proper direction. By repeating to live in the first method, we unintentionally condition our children to give more importance to the don'ts.

'Don't come late' vs 'Come by 9 am.'

'Don't waste time on social media' vs 'Use social media discreetly.'

'Haven't you understood what I said?' vs 'Do you want me to repeat it so that it is clear?'

'Don't watch TV' vs 'Read a storybook.'

'Don't eat sweets' vs 'Eat fruits'

'Don't throw them away' vs 'Keep them safe.'

'Don't bring toys to school' vs 'Play with your toys at home.'

Society constantly finds faults in everyone and doesn't hesitate to point them out. However, it doesn't talk much about the good. If we are to measure, the number of things we are asked 'not to do' outweigh the number we are allowed to do.

Similarly, 'Stopping what we don't like' outweighs 'Doing what we like'. In this approach, the 'No' trait develops strongly gets seated within us as our most natural response. As a result, our brain thinks ten times before saying a 'Yes' even for a simple task, although we can do it. Over time, we feel happy and secure in saying 'No'. Family, society, religions, and faiths focus majorly on the 'No' part.

'Yes' is a positive perspective. It indicates self-confidence. It is a medicine that keeps us in awareness. 'Yes' is an attitude that makes even the impossible achievable. 'Yes' is our first step of faith that we can do it. It is the realisation of our inner capability.

Acceptance and Consent

Saying 'Yes' to everything without even thinking about it like a bull is not what a 'Yes' means. 'Yes' means giving consent not acceptance. In acceptance, there is an ego hidden behind. Acceptance clarifies our relationship with others. Whereas in consent, there is open-mindedness and zero ego. It indicates our condition with our mind. It flows happily aligned to the stream of life. There is only cooperation but no conflict. That is why it saves time and effort.

'No' doesn't mean saying 'no' when asked if a marigold looks like a rose. Likewise, 'no' doesn't mean saying 'no' to something we do not know of.

In hatred, both sides try to become strong and adamant. They strengthen themselves. One needs a reason for it. One needs logic and analysis as well. Hate could lead to conflict. 'Yes' is unanimous. It is much beyond a superconductor and conserves immense energy. 'Yes' means merging. It merges with oneself. Nature, and the universe making the world a happy place.

We think that 'Yes' is the opposite of'No'. The nature of'Yes' is so vast that it includes 'No' as a part of it, just like darkness is part of the light. That is, the moment the lights are off, darkness is known. Similarly, a 'No' should merge with a 'Yes'. Only then, life can be complete.

When we consider 'Yes' and 'No' as separate entities, we turn into multifaceted personalities. Crossing 'No' to merge with 'Yes' should be like a droplet mixing with the ocean, which leads to merging ourselves as one with the universe.

So, how do we cross 'No' to reach 'Yes'?

Following are a few techniques.

Say 'No' to what we shouldn't do

It is to say 'No' to any work that goes against your nature, values, health, and ambitions. Live with your nature. If something comes your way that doesn't match your personality, say no to it. For example, we don't have the habit of smoking, drinking, and gambling. When someone offers, say no to it. When we say yes to our frame of mind or nature, we automatically say no to what harms us.

Say 'No' to what we want to avoid

Some actions against our moral values, time, and goals are usually from a lousy companionship—for instance, going to movies and passing the time in gossip falls under this category. So, let's say no to such unfavourable activities. When we say yes to our life's path, all those unfavourable ones will go away by themselves.

Say 'Yes' to what you should do

There is always that small adage or proverb that says 'yes' to what we should do. Let us list all those actions to which we said no over the last two days and today. Let us analyse them. To our surprise, we will find that 90% of those we said 'no' to are what we can comfortably do. However, we are not doing it. Why?

For instance, your mom asked you to go to the supermarket and get some vegetables. Dad asked for some help with his office work. Your teacher advised learning to use a computer. The physical training instructor wanted you to know badminton. The college wants you to participate in oration and essay writing competitions. A blind person asked to take her to a given address. A friend asked you to apply for some vacant jobs in the banking sector. For various reasons, you said 'no' to all of them. Even if we orally didn't say a 'no', not doing them is as good as saying no to them.

Psychologists devised 'Offer - Block - Accept' games to face such issues. Let us evaluate the problems mentioned above. We can do all of them. But, first, let us look at why we declined them in the first place.

- How is it beneficial to me?
- The fear of failing.
- Fear of what others think of me.
- Fear of public speaking.

For all the above reasons, there is one common attribute which is lack of self-confidence. Additionally,

- It shows that we are anxious about the outcome.
- We are unable to come out of our comfort zone.
- Since childhood, we have been conditioned to say 'no' to most things.

We clearly said 'no' for the above-said reasons. But, what would we do if we knew that we would win? Maybe, we would have taken them up if we knew that they were beneficial.

What harm can happen to us if we fail to do it? What will happen if people laugh at us when we talk on the stage? Have you thought about what good could happen to you if you did? What is the loss we incur in failing after attempting? What did we gain by not attempting? When we say 'yes' to all those we can do, there is a possibility of unforeseeable opportunities that can open before us. That 'yes' can have the potential to change our life too.

The majority of our activities are mechanical. If we analyse our daily lives, our involvement is not there in most of our works. Our relationships, routine, varied situations, and responses....!n this way, there are so many decisions we make with minimal awareness. The majority are produced mechanically. We are like the monkeys played by the juggler of conditioning. We are told what to do and what not to do from childhood. Family, society, and religion constantly show us our mistakes. As a result, we believe that we are incorrect and incomplete. Deep inside, we feel sad that we are not living up to somebody's expectations.

Do you know who is the main one that criticises us?
It is us.

Do you know who is the last one that praises us?
This is again us only.

We are in constant pursuit of becoming something. In that pursuit, we mainly look at our mistakes. But why are we ignoring the fact that nothing is perfect in this world?

Just as we have variety and diversity in animals, birds, trees, and plants, we also have distinctiveness.

Every individual is unique. This means no two individuals are alike. Yet, we constantly try to be like others. So, we lose our identity. Conditioning since childhood is the main reason for this self-criticism.

We all have come onto this Earth with distinct personalities. When our traits, strengths, capabilities, weaknesses are part of it, why don't we accept that? To accept doesn't mean to become static or muted. On the contrary, to accept is to appreciate ourselves.

Are we some kind of puppets in others' hands?

We always think of what others think of us. We expect that our parents, teachers, and society should praise us. We keep trying for that. To get their positive opinion, we change opinions about ourselves. We see ourselves through their spectacles.

We need to have a definite idea about ourselves. That should be the seed to our self-confidence.

Say 'Yes' to Parents

Many of us feel wrong about the conditions we are born with. We want our parents to be in a certain way.

In some families, the father could be a drunkard. For various reasons, parents could've been divorced. Even if both love each other, there could be financial problems. We see others and their conditions and dream of having them and their upbringing for ourselves. We think we could have been better if we had such an ambience and facility.

Like this, we have many complaints against our parents. So, we know now why we don't like their words and build negativity with them.

Many of our traits are inherited from our parents. So, condemning them is equivalent to condemning ourselves. If you observe, all those who do not want to be like their parents end up being like them. Therefore, we lose our power in disapproving of them.

However, if we accept them, we will imbibe new values and identities. There are many reasons for which we should be grateful to our parents. So let us say 'Yes' to all of them.

A State of Mind beyond Circumstances

Human beings are social by nature. Humans got their history through inheritance. Their culture is flowing through generations.

Favourable or unfavourable customs and traditions prevalent in the family and society will influence them. Irrespective of the country, there will be inequalities in any organisation, family, or individual. However, man should not succumb to these situations. They should not blame society or their families for their current state.

Know that our present mind has more effect on us than our past. For instance, in Kashmir, a Hindu woman and a Muslim woman gave birth to two children simultaneously. By mistake, both these children got interchanged at birth. Now, tell me, will the customs and traditions of the Muslim child living in the Hindu family be that of the Hindu or the Muslim family? Likewise, what about the Hindu child growing up in a Muslim family?

Therefore, let us accept all the circumstances around us. Let us put a full stop to all those thoughts that expect the past differently. We can't change the past. Nor can we erase regions, races, religions, and castes. So, what's the point of cribbing about them? Let's say 'yes' to them. Only then can the present open its doors for us. Disappointment and depression will disappear like passing clouds.

Are we different from 'Sophia' in relationships?

Face and voice recognition might be new to the technological revolution but not to humans. A human remembers everything about his known people and things. The mind analyses and organises all this information in a specific pattern.

Whenever something about the person or thing comes to his mind, the brain will fetch everything about him or it. That is why we evade people we don't like. We don't feel like talking to some people. And with some, we wish for friendship. So we answer correctly to what someone is asking.

When someone asks. 'Where does the tiger stay?', we say it lives in the forest but won't say Ramesh is in America. That's because we answer according to the question and the person asking. The moment we know who is calling us over the phone, our style and etiquette change immediately. We tend to vent out our anger on someone due to someone else. This is because the mind stores and processes every piece of information, just like a computer. In the same way. the robot that the man creates speaks like the man. It does all the work. A robot called 'Sophia' has also taken the citizenship of Saudi Arabia.

Humans are distinct from Sophia. If a human wishes, he can free himself of his past. He can reduce the influence of his unconsciousness and increase the impact of his awareness, and live happily. He can say 'yes' to his conflicts with his neighbours and move forward. He can become an observer of himself and stop complaining about things around him.

If you keenly analyse our responses to certain people, they result from our built-in prejudices against them. Its intensity is mostly not related to the situation on hand but with past events.

Many times, we expect others to behave in a certain way. However, let us accept them as they are. Let us understand that even others' behaviour results from their unconsciousness, just as our behaviour is a result of our unawareness. Therefore, let us stay beyond the influences of prejudices and accept them as they are. When we cannot get along with some, let us not blame anybody or anything. Then, we won't be hurt by the separation. The negative feelings about someone will disappear like bubbles in the water.

Emotions are like horses.

If we are good riders, we will make our journey happy.

If we drop the harness, they will drop us down.

If we oppress them, they will suppress you.

If we throw them on others, they will hit us back.

That is why let us say 'yes' to our emotions. Whenever we go through a surge of emotions, let us accept and say that we are emotionally charged and challenging. That's enough.

We will take responsibility for our feelings. That's when our likes and dislikes will open doors to exit in no time. Whenever anyone behaves in a way that makes us angry, let us accept that the source of anger lies in us, not in others. In acceptance alone, our anger evaporates. We will not be trapped in the reasons that our mind shows us.

Thoughts are the parent to the feelings. Matter becomes the foundation for thoughts. Matter includes a person, an item, a subject, or a situation. When we attach our thoughts to the issue, it results in feelings. The feeling is more subtle than the thought. Our feelings change with our thoughts. And our emotions generate more thoughts. For example, the death of a relative is an incident. The consequences of his death and his actions in the past kindle thoughts in us. As a result, sorrow happens. There is no place for sadness when we learn to separate the incident from the thought.

Let us say 'yes' to change by leaving our comfort zone. Like a parrot in a cage, we have also built an enclosure of comfort around us.

We have organised many more like these for our happiness: a life partner, a family, friends, house, vehicle and so on. We plan with the future in mind. There is security in comfort. There is a definiteness in known things. So, we are frightened of change, as it takes us from known to unknown.

Change is the indicator of loveliness. It is dynamic. If we start saying 'yes' to all the changes in our lives, we won't be frightened to lose something. The moment we accept change, we will say goodbye to conditions like 'Ohh! This should not happen to me: it would have been nice: had it been this way[1]. We will only open doors for new opportunities when we say 'yes' to change. New options give way to new experiences. In this way, the fear of uncertainty will wither away. Life will become lively with rejuvenation.

If we have to reach the world of 'yes', we must change the direction from the outer world to the inner world. In that light, we can see ourselves and our life with clarity.

Awareness

Let us observe the web of 'NOs' because of our negative outlook. Just by watching and accepting, it melts away.

What is our heart saying to us? Is it saying 'yes'? Or 'no'? Knowing what is happening in our thoughts, feelings, and processes is what awareness means.

Acceptance

We resist our emotions that say, 'I don't want this. I don't like this'. As a result, we succumb to psychological conflict.

So, let us accept them as they are. This acceptance breaks the logic and argument that our mind makes.

Let Go

Inculcate a let go attitude instead of holding onto problems forever and get out of the mind's chess of complaints.

Responsibility

We are the owners of our life. We are responsible for our joy and sorrow. It is not other people or circumstances around. So let us own all the good and bad in our life. As a result, our life comes back from others' folds into our hands. And travels from 'no' to 'yes'.

Yes

Self-confidence increases for those who take responsibility for their lives. In that, we hear the song 'yes'. The perspective of 'yes' enables the growth of creativity in us. The creativity that started with a 'yes' wears the wings of self-confidence and flies in the experiences of the sky to touch the stars of victory. It will cut off all negative bonding and breathe in the air of freedom.

Accepting every individual and situation in this world and making our lives happy is called 'yes'. Nature has many things for us. It gives us constantly. Let's say 'yes' to all those which Nature bestows us. That 'Yes' should flow from our breath.

In the words of E.E.Cummings, a well-known American author, columnist, and painter.

Yes is a world
and in this world of yes
live (skilfully curled)
all worlds

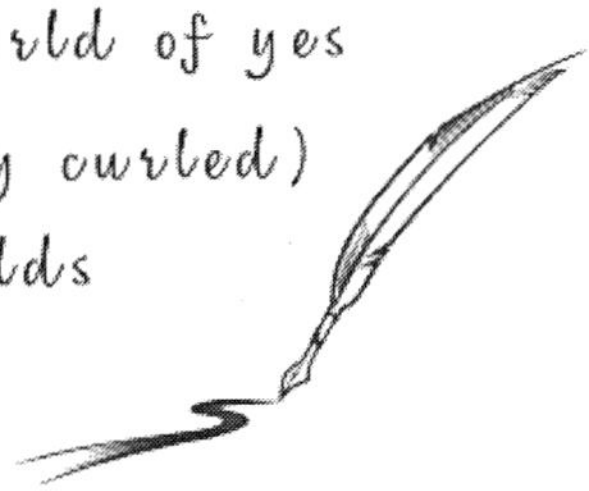

❑

Images

Images are the most influential catalysts in our life. They are the drivers that ride on our senses and moods/inclinations. They are the windows to the outside world and the keys that open doors to our thoughts.

Physically we are listening through ears and seeing through eyes. However, we hear and see through what our mind has already stored. At the outset, both sounds and visuals look normal. Both together form images in our minds. They are no less than the supernatural powers that control our lives. Be it relationships, personality development, or professional life, images dictate every phase and aspect of our lives. One can lead a happy life on careful observation of sounds and visuals.

There is an image behind a sound. Be it nouns like tree, hill, land; be it pronouns like I, you, she; be it verbs like eating, playing, drawing.... whatever be the sound, there is a meaning behind them. Behind that meaning is an image. Behind the image is an experience.

Experience is related to the past. Past is a feeling. We tend to note all those that come under our area of experience - people, things, incidents, and situations. We name them like a hill, an elephant, and so on. For example, we called the tall thing on the plane a hill, and we said the one with a trunk, large ears, big tusks and a massive elephant body. The moment we hear that name, its picture comes to our mind. However, if we call a hill an elephant, people will think that we are mindless.

Knowledge is also related to the past. We impart our knowledge to the infants by showing the visuals of people and things around while uttering the names. That is how we impart knowledge.

However, if we were to interchange the names of elephant and hill, we need to change the experiences. For that, we need to go into the past. But, to go into the past, we have to unlearn first. For this reason, it is easy to learn anything quickly during childhood.

Children grasp things very quickly. On the other hand, adults face situations and things with their experience. For example, a swimming coach has to teach swimming to a child and an adult. The adult already knew about the countryside swimming. Yet, while the child could learn the proper techniques and strokes in thirty days, the adult takes longer than six months. That's because the adult should first unlearn the traditional methods he knew to learn the new techniques.

This observation proves that it is more difficult to forget what we learn than to learn something new.

Is there a sound without an image?

Some express good, evil, anger, and irritation. However, there's a scene behind that expression. In that scene, there's a visual.

We don't interpret a laughing person as angry or a crying person to be happy, right? We can't see the air. We don't even know what it looks like. However, there's an experience with the air. We know that the one blowing and the one breathing is air. Through the swaying of the leaves and the flying of the balloons, we try to visualise air. Likewise, we try to bring into our experience the feel of electricity, gravity, magnetism, and energy.

We haven't seen sweetness, saltness, sourness and so on. However, when we eat something of these tastes, we recollect and visualise how we used to feel.

Whenever we listen to an unknown aspect, we try to relate it to the known. Hence, we connect it with the image.

There is no meaning to the sounds Kee Kaa Pee Paa. They don't have a visual. Yet, we relate these sounds to something we know or some language we have heard. But, of course, they don't create any visuals in us until we attach a meaning to it. Even animals make similar sounds. So, we remember those sounds and recollect the respective animals when we hear these sounds. While focusing on the tone, those learning music save the feeling in an image. They focused on the seven notes Sa, Ri, Ga, Ma, Pa, Da, Ni while singing.

Is there an image without a sound?

There are no sounds to our gestures, codes, expressions, and feelings. Yet, they are all visuals and have a meaning behind them. Visuals form into memory. Our memories are stored as images in our minds. For the mentally challenged, all these images will be shattered. Hence, they can't recognise anyone. They can't compare anything. That means the thread or connection between the object and memory and between the object and image is broken. The necessary bridge collapsed. As a result, they won't apply the images as others do. And they cannot use the words the way others do.

Similarities and Differences are also images

Images function as powerhouses of thoughts.

'Why can't you be stable like your brother?' says the mother. 'Why don't you study well like your friend Suresh?', says the father. 'If you don't know how to work, why don't you learn from your colleague?' says the officer.

When you compare yourself with someone, the image of that person is there in your mind. Even the one who is hearing it also creates a picture in his mind. As a result, the listener understands and visualises how he should be so that mom likes him, understands how to study so that dad becomes happy, and understands how he should work so that the officer approves it. Here, he tries to visualise and imprint information of all those ideals he needs to follower imitate. With that, he starts comparing those ideals and competing to be like them or better than them. The concept of following the role model is of this nature only.

Time is an image

Time is a thought. Thought is an image.

When we look at ourselves in the past or the future, we live in a world of visuals. The hope of 'what do we want to become in the future' and regrets about 'what we haven't been in the past' is always in the form of visuals in our minds.

All these thoughts create images in our brains. Images are the things of the past. Our thoughts may travel in the past or future, but our images are based on the past. So, these images operate in all our assessments on 'how are we today?' to 'how were we in the past?' and 'how should we be in the future?'.

Sweet memories and bitter experiences are always in sounds and visuals. Whenever someone makes us sad, we recollect everything in the past that hurt us. That is why our reaction to the current incident is usually disproportionate to the event because our response results from the accumulation of visuals of the past. So, we end up giving a big punishment even for a small mistake. We can observe this phenomenon even in judicial judgements. If the incident is similar to an experience, the impact will be 1+1 = 11 instead of 2. Similarly, if the experiences are distinct, then the effect will be 1-1 = -1, 0

Opinions are also images

The opinions we form of others stay as visuals in our minds. We categorise people as good, evil, rich, poor, greedy and temperamental based on the images we formed about them.

When we say -

'He's not the kind who listens to anybody',

'There's no use in asking this officer',

... we express our opinions about them.

Here, the images function as a vehicle to the opinion. These images act as stumbling blocks in human relationships.

Thoughts and Images

Thoughts are the parents of images. A thought means a feeling. It is a reaction to the memories stored.

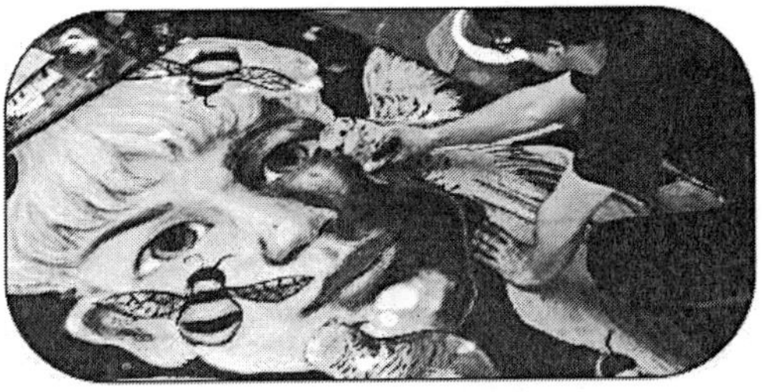

A painter expresses his ideas with a paintbrush that others see through his artwork.

Likewise, a writer does it with his pen, where others see his thoughts in his writings.

Castes, religions, races, countries, virtues, and justices reflect our beliefs only. Behind our regulations, ideologies, debates, and obedience lie our feelings. Behind that feeling is an image. In that way, our feelings enter our minds as visuals representing good-bad, joy-sorrow, and likes-dislikes. As a result, differences, contradictions, conflicts, and wars occur between two opposite images rather than two opponents.

If we observe this imaginary world created by our thoughts with attention, our minds can no longer trick us. When we are entirely calm inside, we can see our thoughts clearly. Our doubts, opinions, and feelings disappear in that clarity. Similarly, visuals initiate our thoughts.

'It is impossible to think without an image' in Aristotle's words.

Images touch all corners of our life. Most people submerge their lives in this ocean of sounds and visuals. Few people dive in it and swim out successfully. Here arises a doubt. Will there be a life untouched by the images? We can say a 'no. Does that mean we have to surrender to our pictures? It doesn't have to be.

Images help us in various ways. We need to find ways and means to make use of them. However, through methods like meditation, we can reduce the negative impact of images to lead a happier life. It's just like harnessing the tides to produce energy.

Images of Success and Failure

Success and failure are succeeded by emotions. These emotions are the results of our experiences. These experiences are stored as images in the brain. We feel happy thinking about the successes. Failures create fear within us. These feelings take roots from experience.

The claps, the felicitations, the appreciations, and the awards are symbols of success. We connect success with these images. Imagine a different picture of success. Visualise what feelings we might get when we face criticisms, abuses, and rejections soon after a victory. Then what feelings do we associate with victory?

We expect an outcome for our work. We have an image of the outcome. When the result doesn't match our vision, we feel disappointed. Then, we look for reasons. However, the thought that we get 'had we done it some other way, then the outcome would have been something else' is also an image. For example, athletes participating in the Olympics visualise how fast they have to run to cover a particular distance and at a specific time. While correcting mistakes, they strive to reach the target.

Images of likes and dislikes

We form likes and dislikes because of our experiences. The same product can be associated with both like and dislike, dependent on the incident. For example, we bought a mobile phone. We use it and bring it into our experience. We see another new phone in the market. Now, we start to imagine that phone and want to own it. We don't stop there. Then another phone. This is how we end up with many wishes. We acquire more gadgets than required. We arrange varieties of tablets, laptops at home.

Even before we use them properly, we start looking for new products. Yet, we hardly use them to their full potential. Many things are lying in our houses that we have not used once. In this way, we move from one object to another, influenced by the visuals. These objects need not necessarily be electronic gadgets. It could be clothes, cars, houses, books and so on. We compare the things we have and what we wish to have. As a result, we create likes and dislikes, satisfaction and dissatisfaction. We chase after likes. In this way, we go round and round the merry-go-round of our desires.

Reasons and results are also images

Whenever we do some work, want to do it, or when we are doing it, we expect an outcome. So, we imagine how that outcome can become a positive feeling. However, when the result is otherwise, we feel dejected. We find reasons. Then, we devise solutions on how that should have been in retrospection.

Experience is an image

If we notice our daily life, we can categorise all people, animals, things, and places into two segments.

- Those that we know
- Those that we do not know

What we know will stay as an image in our minds. That is why the moment we hear of neem; we recollect the experience of eating that bitter taste. When we ask how jaggery tastes, we immediately say 'it is sweet', and our mouth waters remembering the experience of tasting it. That means when we are eating; it becomes an experience. When this experience goes into our memory, it stays as an image. In this way, we recognise different things, people, and places from our experiences.

Our experiences guard us against moving away from known to unknown territories. However, until we make an effort, we don't bring new things, places, or people into our experience.

An effort has expectations of the outcome. When the result is doubtful, the action takes a step backwards.

The one who puts effort and enter into an unknown world without expectations are called experts or veterans.

Chilean poet Pablo Neruda wrote...

'You start dying slowly,

If you do not change your life

When you are not satisfied with your job, or with your love,

If you do not risk what is safe for the uncertain,

If you do not go after a dream,

If you do not allow yourself

At least once in your lifetime,

To run away from sensible advice...'

Images in relationships

Images have a tremendous influence on all our relationships. Relations are deeply rooted in the emotions felt by them. We talk to others with an opinion in mind. Likewise, even when someone talks to us, they also carry their opinion about us. These premeditated opinions become barriers to our relationship.

We don't get to see each other past these images. To know the person we are talking to, we must cross these past images.

Similarly, even the person talking to us also sees us through the images. Our imaginative forms supersede the actual arrangements. What we already know overrides what we see now. As a result, there is discordance in our relationships.

For example, the moment we say 'I know Ravi', it means that we already have an opinion about Ravi. We know only the images we formed about Ravi's good, bad, lavish, or spendthrift qualities. These images play a major role in our relationships — husband-wife, parents-children, teacherstudent, friends, neighbours, and relatives. Therefore, we reciprocate based on what others did to us. Not just that, we reciprocate our helping nature or love to others based on what was given back to us.

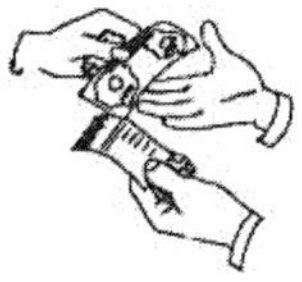

But, tell me, how long will these calculative relations stand?

Is love possible among these images?

How stable can the relationships trapped in the convolution of preconceived notions be?

Can relations endure without love?

That is why let us build our connections by keeping aside images that stand as hindrances among us. Sweetness will flow like a river in our relationships only when we accept others with a crystal-clear heart.

Fake images

Fake images are fictitious. Yet, we believe them as facts. These counterfeit images will influence how we see our past, present and future behaviour. We hear many concocted stories about incidents and personalities on social media platforms like Facebook, WhatsApp, YouTube, and Twitter. These get imprinted in our brains.

For example - we see Former American President Barack Obama shaking hands with former Iran President Mahmoud Ahmadinejad; pictures of George Bush with baseball pitcher Roger Clemens during the Hurricane calamity. Factually, these two incidents did not happen but have been processed as facts to the public.

Similarly, we come across a lot of media attention around temples, mosques, and religious books that lead to religious strife. There's no reality in them. There's also much fuss around food and drinks. Seeing them, we choose to follow or avoid some foods or beverages. In this way, we form opinions about others after listening to or seeing such scenes. We don't check the authenticity of these sayings. Instead, we see and test others through such incidents.

Language was born from the sound. It has given words to feelings. Feelings were born before the speech. Language is essential to express emotions. Feelings arise out of sounds and visuals. We hear sounds. We see visuals. These two are indeed difficult in our life. In fact, the effects of hearing and seeing are one and the same.

By the way, what is seeing?

It is like pure milk after removing water from the milk. Seeing is observation. Observation without the mind. We all see nature, creatures, and things with past experiences. Initially, we doubt a rose if we see it in green colour. Don't we? That's because we have an impression of a rose in red colour. Similarly, suppose we see a curled moustache guy sitting before us. In that case, we assume that he is highly temperamental, so we avoid talking to him.

We have been forming opinions from what we see and hear from childhood. That's how we create them as images in our minds. But we don't stop there. We design imaginations about the future too. In this way, we see the outside world through our internal world.

We hear the sound. Then we connect it to the meaning. Hence, meaning is nothing but an image. Thus, we listen to the other person with the vision in our mind. Because of these images, there's a gap between the speaker and the listener.

Unable to handle her husband's abuses, a woman goes and sits alone in a park. There, she can't listen to the sounds of the birds or the trees. Instead, all that she listens to is her husband's abuse. In this way, we listen to our inner world more than the external world.

Sound and vision meet at a point. That point is an image.

When we study, both listening and seeing happen.

These two meet in conversations and in relations too. When we dialogue with someone, we are mainly influenced by our past experiences. These images are perceptions; when two people talk together, it's not the people talking together, but their images.

Where is the possibility of hearts meeting amidst the images?

Over and above, these images are obstructing our communication. We make judgements like good-bad, like-dislike, and beautiful-ugly. Only when we go beyond these meeting points can we remove the obstacles between man vs man, man vs nature. There is no ego of T in that place. There, beauty dances energetically, and love blossoms.

Ne need to be aware of the images created by our minds to get past these. Suppose we observe them keenly, vacuum forms. In that vacuum, whatever we listen to and see will be beautiful.

Let us observe with our complete self.

Let us remove the curtains of feelings between us and others and see clearly.

Let's listen and see with complete attention. There won't be any scope for delusion when we watch something with that full attention. There's no room for memory or knowledge because we go beyond the images.

When there is no T in that vacuum feeling, we will see beauty in exuberance behind those images.

Interestingly, our minds won't interfere in those images. There won't be authoritarians of our past feelings. Instead, we can form a direct relationship with anyone and anything in that space. Then we truly make our life an ocean of joy.

❑

Loneliness

'Man is neither as social as a honey bee nor as solitary as a lion.'

How has loneliness started playing hide and seek with our innocent children? Why did this poisonous snake engulf the youth that should be exuberant with enthusiasm as their spirit? What made the dark cloud of loneliness cover the householder who has been driving the boat of life with ease? Why should our elderly parents, who enlighten us with their elixir of experiences and knowledge, spend their time in the same darkness of loneliness?

Come. Let us understand how this thief entered our homes. Let us recognise how it is robbing our happiness by hiding as water in milk. Let us analyse how it doesn't let us climb the ladder by continuously swallowing us like the serpents in the game of Snake & Ladder.

Finally, let us observe our inner world to identify the invisible causes and not the apparent reasons to eliminate this contagion from our lives.

•••• loneliness of affection

A human being is primarily a dependent being. He depends on other beings. Initially, he relies on nature and then on other beings. Relationships and mutual exchange have become part of his life. He created distinct groups such as castes, religions, races, communities, regions and countries. In this way, the man moved from the human race to specific groups.

Man has become a servant to machines in the current market economy. As a result, his life became increasingly questionable without these machines. In this way, from the womb to the tomb, a man's life is dependent on something or the other.

Life is like a game for children. We introduce learning institutes like schools and colleges at such a playful age. In that strange world, the child naturally looks for friends. However, he finds only those who breathe in and out the air of competition.

Competition is Like an Unquenchable Thirst.

Leisure is an Unapproachable Sweet Grape.

Even if our children did find it, parents come in between to snatch it away from them. With parents' intervention, children end up making friendships with digital screens. In that way, the screens started to shadow their lives like dark clouds. So, they search for happiness in animations and cartoons. It is the age where they smile with flowers. It is the time when they play with the birds and animals joyfully. But we have restricted their lives to closed walls. Today, if there is even a minor power cut, it seems as if a powerful force swallowed their world. We have forced them to drink the darkness of loneliness when they ideally should be playing with the sky as the limit and all nature as their playground. Tablets and televisions have dug a bottomless pit, not letting our children meet each other. This state is the 'loneliness of affection'.

loneliness of association ....

The youth are oscillating between jealousy and ego. While some are raging with ambitions, others are getting used to laziness. Some are submitting completely to pleasures. For all these types, day and night are the same.

Ambitious people don't accept the growth of fresh foliage into yellow. In contrast, the lazy ones are old by birth. For the latter, gossip is their nutrition.

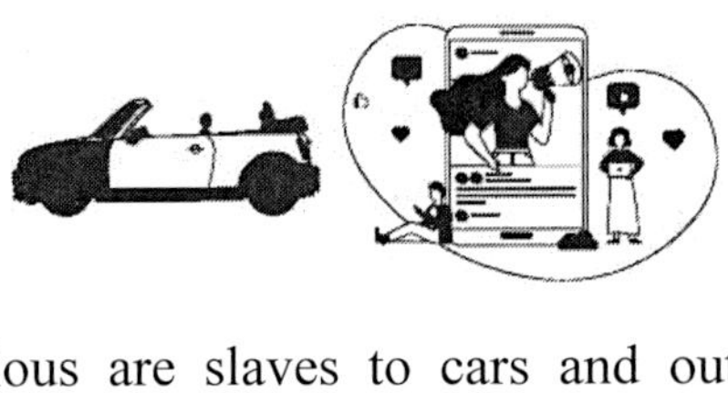

The luxurious are slaves to cars and outings. And the majority of the youth spend their time within the prisons of social mediums. They eat and sleep on social media only.

This state is the 'loneliness of association'.

•••• loneliness of pastimes

For householders, television serials have become a daily dose of addiction. The blue screen has chained their legs, and they lost interest in talking to their neighbours.

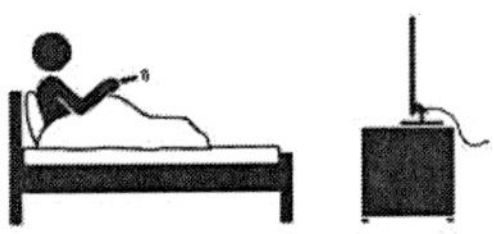

Some stroll around in all directions for time to pass and spend in endless chats. For them, it is fun to talk about others and spread rumours.

Some men spend their lifetime gambling and consuming alcohol. They like pastimes that hallucinate their minds. This state is the 'loneliness of pastimes'.

The older generation spent time chanting the shlokas from the Bhagavad Gita, discussing epics and scriptures.

They were also used to being involved in charitable activities. And they were empathetic to each other.

technology induced loneliness ••••

For many, mobile phones have become a part of their mind. As if two hands aren't enough, now they have four phones in addition to laptops and tablets.

Though there are thousands of people in the bus stations, railway stations and airports, each one is entirely immersed in their cell world. They keep themselves busy chatting on social media, YouTube and apps. On average, today's youth spend ten hours on their screens.

On the other hand, 60% of people spend six hours on digital platforms globally.

According to the research conducted by the University of Maryland, youth are adversely getting affected by mobile phones. It makes them laggard, restless, depressed and thereby losing interest in building relationships. They are getting distanced from sleep and smile.

So, naturally, despite being in a crowd, they feel lonely. This state is the 'technology-induced loneliness'.

It is ideal to be self-sufficient. However, in old age, one loses needed life energies. They are treated as burdens to friends and family. Children ignore their words and get irritated with their advice.

A famous saying goes like this - 'the asking mouth has no value in front of the giving hands'.

Adults get frustrated with those elders that depend upon them. In one research conducted, 20% of the people above 60 years are experiencing the highest form of loneliness. That is why there is an increasing demand for old-age homes. This is the 'loneliness of old age'.

Domestic loneliness ....

When it comes to the matters of the home, the situation is even more dreadful. All stay together in the same house but aren't together. Though their bodies are near each other, the distance between their hearts is so large that they can't stand talking to each other. This may happen in society and countries also.

Some sections of society are neglected and alienated. Some migrants were looked down on and isolated. Here, the dominant ones exploit the others in every way. The exploited people live in isolation and constant fear. This type of loneliness is called 'Domestic loneliness'.

.... loneliness of societal insecurity

In the name of castes & religions, races & communities, styles & countries, the gap between every two human beings is increasing. Every group creates its own distinct Cod. Leave aside the need to talk; one group fights with the other group.

Amidst thousands of Cods, each Cod also has to experience loneliness.

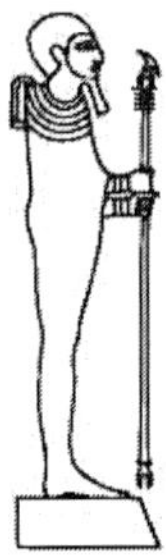

Human beings guard their Cods to ensure they don't get a break from being lonely. Such people don't stop with colonising Cods; they reinstate and imprison their gurus and freedom fighters' statues and paint them colourfully in the name of ideologies. They raise rivalry between their ideologies and create unnecessary conflict. These statues endlessly guard so that no one crosses the boundaries of religions, castes, and races.

Self-respect has superseded the happiness of the soul. To maintain self-respect, they have to do continuous worship and processions to their Cods. Because of such public displays, we have created enmity among people around us. In this public display, some are being alienated. For some, the shades of loneliness are relatively high. This state is the 'loneliness of societal insecurity'.

.... loneliness of geopolitical egos

Nationality has become like a mole to a human. However far we may go and how many so ever oceans we may cross, the identity of nationality will keep us separate. It will ensure to tie us with our nativity and prevent us from mixing with the world. This way, nationality binds one like a rope that ties a pet animal to a pillar. Nationality instils patriotism so that man doesn't run away from its fold.

Tell me, a man revving up with patriotism, can he be alone?

Until one is within one's political borders, one believes that the country will support them. The moment an individual crosses the boundaries, they become an expatriate forever. He becomes a loner among strangers. This state is the 'loneliness of geopolitical egos'. The ego of one's nationality and regionalist chauvinism belong to this type only.

The concept of a nation came into existence to remove the fear of one individual against the other. It created law. Under its canopy, the individual breathes the air of freedom and finds relief from hatred and violence to some extent.

As a result, he uses his knowledge and intellect. However, if the nation tries to crush his emotions, he will resist. The nation's intention is not to treat its people as machines or animals.

Man will pull down the governments if they behave otherwise. Over time, he embraced democracy that respects his decisive power and intelligence. However, some won't take responsibility for their actions. A nation that respects its people's thoughts is a blessing to itself and its people.

On the other hand, although scholars and intellectuals seek solitude by choice, the disease of loneliness doesn't touch even slightly. This lot enjoys the journey in their respective creative worlds and converse in a world they create.

All these types of loneliness are man's creations.

Loneliness doesn't confine to any specific age. It hurts like a thorn in the initial stage, and then it harms as it advances.

Strangely enough, loneliness has given us social gatherings. Unfortunately, however, the same social groups provide loneliness to the man.

And by the way, why does a man want to stay in a group?

A group gives shelter, security and power to an individual. It is as if you get more light when you stand out among a thousand stars. A man stays compliant to these groups' values, customary practices, and predispositions. In this compliance, he finds comfort. In comfort, he finds security. As a result, he won't risk stepping out of this well-trodden path. Like a tree in the forest, he merges his identity with the group.

A group is like a playing field. It's like a lab. It's like a theatre. He plays his role in the group. At the same time, he wants to show his individual talent. A group shares happiness. At times, it suppresses individual happiness. Croup stresses uniformity. Individual struggles for diversity. So, there is a conflict. A man feels singled out and lonely because of this conflict between him and the group.

By joining a group, one must lose something to fit into the rules and regulations. However, so long as one benefits from the group, an individual stays inside that group. These benefits can be in the form of societal, financial, spiritual, or recognition.

As he becomes one in the forest, 'I, me, mine' seedlings arise. These lead him to think about what he has lost by joining a group.

He tries to convince people around him. He pleads for their approval. Remember, it is always your inner fragrance that spreads around you. It's invisible. It doesn't need any publicity. People won't get influenced by our appearances or by our arguments.

When the man starts to feel the sourness of discontent, he begins to explore new tastes. He undergoes an inner conflict in deciding between leaving the benefits he has from the group and the inability to get what he desires.

Some people exit their existing groups in the name of spirituality and liberation. However, they either form new groups or join like-minded groups.

Some come out of the existing relationships and prepare themselves to live alone in caves or the Himalayas.

Unable to understand the silence of the lonely caves, these men transform them into 'Ashrams' and 'Mathas/Monasteries'. In this way, the man who escaped from groups again moves towards groups.

Some individuals often go unbalanced between what they desire and what's happening around them. So, they trot towards addictions or suicide—the majority compromise on what's available instead of succumbing to addictions or suicides. There are also those unhappy turbulent souls who find solace in drugs and alcohol.

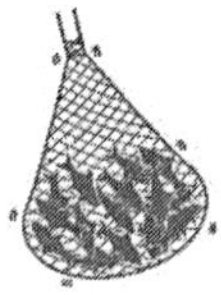

Overall, we observe that a man feels like a trapped fish in a net, unable to get out of the group nor surrender to its specifications.

Our mental state alone decides our state of affairs. Keeping in mind the situations around us, we have to keep adjusting our mental state like a needle in a compass. However wealthy or intelligent one may be, one cannot be happy if one doesn't dynamically ignite the lamp of consciousness to the changing circumstances. Such a man is a loner even among a bunch of friends.

How can an Indian staying in America who is constantly looking for his homeland s food habits and tastes be happy?

The body roams around. It does all the activities necessary for life. It sees, listens, feeds, comforts and experiences all.

But the soul remains at home. It's like the Sun in the solar system. The wise man stays at home, whereas the layman runs from pillar to pole, ignoring his soul.

Does a man ever be lone? Or alone? Man is with his heart at a point in time. And he is with society in the next moment. He lives in the past or the future. And comes to the present at intervals. The reality is that he is not single. Neither he lives lonely or alone. The relationship between a man and a group is like that of birds on a tree.

Can we imagine the existence of a human without a society? Constant support to each other and cohabitation are the characteristics of any group. Competition, comparison, and progress are one's nature. When we drive life as a vehicle using the fuel of cooperation, one's journey becomes beautiful.

A group should facilitate the growth of an individual. It should work like the Sun's rays for an individual's physical, mental and spiritual growth.

We teach our children what to do and what not to do. We also teach them what to eat and what not to eat. As a result, they learn to adjust to the ways of society. However, we need to ask them what they want and like. We need to make efforts to find their thoughts and inclinations.

A group should aid as a foundation for the individual to grow like a tree soaring up towards the sky while keeping one's roots firmly in society.

What do we do when we are lonely?

We talk with ourselves. We converse about our problems unidirectionally in the same path and go to the depths of the ocean of sorrow. We blindly follow the saying of our elders - 'Share happiness with others but experience your sorrow alone'. And then, we end up finding the reasons behind our unhappiness, formulate our mindless theories, and carry the burden of it all.

We go breathless in the deluge of feelings of being lost, living a meaningless life, neglect, and being outcast by society. Loneliness lives on the problems created by the past rather than on the concern for the future.

To be alone means to believe our own thoughts.
To be lonely means to live single in the world's thoughts.

To be alone means to believe our thoughts. To be lonely means to live single in the world's thoughts.

Aloneness doesn't mean living in isolation; it means living with the heart and being truthful to our hearts.

Desire and anger possess those who are lonely. Lonely minds revolve around problems like a bumblebee. Discontentment, regret, fatigue, sluggishness circle them like wasps.

An individual gets tempted towards pleasures, thinking that they would give relief. As a result, one feels lonely even in a crowd.

In the pursuit of protecting himself from loneliness, an individual mingles and joins with others in the name of worship, rituals and festivals. He attaches something special to each date and celebrates it like a festival. So many days like Valentine's

Day, Mother's Day, and Father's Day find a place in his diaries.

If these celebrations were only to provide relief, it would be like a married woman shuttling between in-laws' home and parents' home for comfort from both the house's harassment.

If we are going to live otherwise, we need to know the root cause of our sorrows. With awareness, woes will disappear like clouds. As per Vidura's philosophy (as per a reference in The Mahabharata), four things to avoid when lonely. He described in the following shloka:

एकः स्वादु न भुञ्जीत नैकः सुप्तेषु जागृयात्।
एको न गच्छेदध्वानं नैकश्चार्थान्प्रचिन्तयेत्॥

The shloka means

- one should not enjoy sweets or sumptuous food alone,
- one should not think about strategies alone,
- one should not proceed on a long journey alone,
- and one should not think of gaining wealth alone or not worry alone about acquiring wealth,
- one should not keep himself awake alone while others are sleeping.

Loneliness can bother anyone who belongs to a region, a religion, a community, or a culture. But, for the individual who erases the boundaries of life, the world is one group. For such a universal man, the world is a beautiful garden. His every action beautifully aligns with nature. Neither jealousy, hatred, sorrow or desires would touch him. Nor does fear and anxiety bite him.

As **Ralf Waldo Emerson** said

"It is easy in the world to live after the world's opinion; it is easy in solitude to live after our own, but the great man is he who amid the crowd keeps with perfect sweetness the independence of solitude."

Loneliness can bother anyone who belongs to a region, a religion, a community, or a culture. But, for the individual who erases the boundaries of life, the world is one group. For such a universal man, the world is a beautiful garden. His every action beautifully aligns with nature. Neither jealousy, hatred, sorrow or desires would touch him. Nor does fear and anxiety bite him.

Those who speak their inner voice will become the voice of the world. These are the kind of people who live forever in the heart of the time. Socrates, Plato, Tolstoy, Gandhiji lived by what their hearts taught. Not by what society taught.

We should leave our footprints wherever we walk. For this, we have to walk alone. Walking on the steps of society explains nothing.

Time has its dynamics. With time, change happens within an individual. This change applies even to groups. That is why when we are trying to understand human relationships from an individual or a group point of view, we should not take them as static. Only when we know relations from the said natural dynamics can we see the truth. We can accept the changes without friction only then.

Human life is a part of nature. Just as mother Nature comprises beauty, pleasures, disasters, and calamities, human life is also a blend of joys and sorrows. If we understand them as mere life experiences, we can attain a steady state. When we live in harmony with nature, why will loneliness haunt us?

Let us remove the darkness of loneliness with the hope of a candle. Then everything will be illuminated. There will be happiness everywhere the mind can traverse. Even the little darkness hiding in a corner, too, has to surrender to this light.

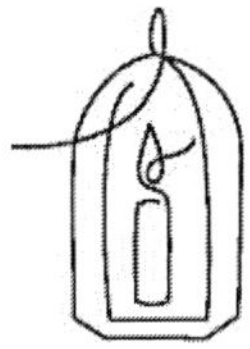

Practice and Creativity

Are Geniuses Born?

'The world called me a genius after I practised fourteen hours a day for 37 years,' said Pablo de Sarasate, a Spanish violin virtuoso, composer and conductor of the Romantic period.

'I fear not the man who has practised 10,000 kicks once, but I fear the man who has practised one kick 10,000 times,' said Bruce Lee, the most influential martial artist of all time.

Srikant, an Intensive Integrated Coaching cum College student, was silently standing when his father consoled his tearful mother. The centre Principal reassured Srikant's parents that their son is intelligent, although his marks don't reflect that. He further said that if Srikanth practises more, he will come in the top hundred ranks in the NEET entrance exam. He corroborated the famous saying that we always hear 'Practice makes a man perfect'. However, the parents were perplexed why an intelligent boy could not fare well.

So, let's get to the point. What makes practice worthwhile? It helps not only in knowing about something but also to preserve the knowledge. We usually know about things we hear, study or happen around us. It could be through our teachers, reading, or experiences. We are essentially reiterating in practice. We are not creating anything new in this exercise.

Can the mind that regularly exercises a specific practice ever supersede itself?

Is it possible to exude creativity when bound by discipline? Doesn't creativity need freedom?

Focus serves like manure for any practice. To be able to concentrate, we need to have a target first. To achieve a target, one requires discipline. When one is disciplined, our desire for something will control the mind.

In a controlled environment, where is the place for creativity? How can one discover anything new when engrossed in one's aspiration, just like how we anchor a ship to reach a particular destination?

How can the mind set itself free to explore other things when it focuses on achieving a definite outcome that follows a defined methodology and routine?

However prominent that goal might be, whatever field (scientific, craftmanship, spirituality) that might be, won't it be similar to marriages bound together with some expectations?

Creativity arises when one is free from the pressure to do or be something.

Can we achieve goodness by practice?

Is someone who constantly practices being good, good?

Is someone who desperately tries to be obedient, obedient?

Our mind should not be a slave to only recall or recap.

If we can leave aside parasites, those who rely on work generally live for three primary objectives:

Those Who Work Without A Goal

Those who work without a goal work only for survival - food, shelter, and clothing. You will find people who study for others' sake in this type. Given a choice, they don't want to. For them, life is a constant burden. So, they helplessly work like a machine.

Theirs is pure physical effort, without gaining happiness. We can compare them with the ploughing bullocks.

Those Who Work With A Goal

Such people work to get something or become something. Their heart is on the outcome, and they direct their work to achieve the desired result.

You can compare this to racecourse horses trained primarily to win in competitions. While their success gives them happiness, it doesn't bring contentment. It's pure emotional effort.

Those Who Work With Joy

Such people work as if they are born to perform. Their very life breath is in it, just like how Pandit Bismillah Khan breathes himself into his Shehnai.

They engross themselves in their efforts. Their focus is on the improvement of their performance. They devotedly pursue to better it every time until they reach the highest possible potential.

These are not the kind of people touched by weariness or boredom. For them, they and their work are no different. It's pure intellectual effort.

For any effective practice, one primarily needs three tools - awareness, target and involvement.

Awareness

Being aware of our thoughts, likes, and strengths.

Target

Creating a target with awareness and working towards it with perseverance.

Involvement

Being immersed in the task at hand is essential to enjoy and relax through the sweetness of work. This alone gives strength to progress through all shortcomings. For this, our mind should be in the present. It should be involved in the process. Then there's only action, no doer.

Not being anxious about the outcome is the natural source of life for practice.

Can anyone stop the result when we put in our efforts? For instance, you will gain energy when you eat nutritious food. If you study well, you will gain knowledge. Who can stop that? By boiling, we get rice to eat for our meals.

Good action arises from good thoughts.

Hence, our focus should be on the work but not the outcome. Instead, we should focus on the techniques in performing the work. Our output will be proportional to our efforts only. Not worrying about the outcome doesn't mean that we have no goals in life. It simply means that we don't give attention to the consequences, which indirectly enslaves us in the desire to possess it.

Observe what happens when you turn your attention from the outcome to the method of work. You will notice that there is no room for stress. But you might wonder, how does that happen?

When our mind focuses on a thing and loses sight of it, it suffers from increased anxiety levels. This anxiety will unnecessarily create opinions and judgements that will hinder our progress. These judgements will decide the direction of our thoughts and destiny as we form strong views on what is good and evil and what is right and wrong. That is why it is essential to review our efforts impartially without becoming judgemental.

Remember, our previous trials should act as a foundation for our future practices at any point in time. Therefore, all these efforts should move on a concrete path.

Having a credit card mentality haunts us like an evil shadow.

We tend to expect quick results without much effort on the path. We dream of acquiring wealth overnight. By sunrise, we want our dreams to come true. We are wrestling with goals within, like how we forcefully boil rice in a pressure cooker. We think we have no time and become highly impatient.

Competitions and comparisons are making us run endlessly. We have started considering nights a waste of time and wishing for nightless days. We have ignored that rest helps us recuperate from weariness and invigorates us to handle the following day's tasks.

However noble our goal might be, our path should be much nobler. Our goals should act as directional guidance for our efforts but not act as demons that block our way. Like our school Principal stated, 'Practice makes a man perfect'. But, in this, what do you mean by 'perfect'? Is there anything perfect? Is that even possible?

We come across various marketing messages like —

'Your life is imperfect without this car',

'This jacket makes you the perfect man.'

In life, too, we chase perfection. A husband looks for perfection in his wife, a teacher in his students and citizens in their leader. Like this, we make others feel that they are not perfect until they meet our expectations.

Has anyone ever achieved perfection?

You might want to say no, but I say 'yes'. We all have

achieved perfection in every phase of life. As a seedling, a plant, a flower, and a fruit.

Perfection is not a statue that
Gets installed once and for all.
It's like a stream.

Practice is not born or reborn. Instead, it is about continuously using one's emotional, intellectual and inherent abilities. It constitutes planning and plans too. The quality of practice prepares us for acquiring many more qualities. While correcting our mistakes, it steers life on a beautiful carpet.

Without practice, where will Sachin Tendulkar be? Can we imagine a Raja Ravi Verma or a Picasso without continuous efforts? What about a Visveswaraya or an Einstein without trials? What do you think the state of a Ratan Tata or a Steve Jobs would be without continuous action?

We see that we do the same thing repeatedly in our jobs. The same thing applies to cooking too. How come we are not getting irritated or bored by doing the same thing repeatedly? Won't repetition discourage our enthusiasm?

Why is despair not bothering us in these repetitions?

If we observe our daily activities, we usually don't bother much about the outcomes. We believe that the results will happen in their natural course and focus on the task. We only see that we follow the process diligently and find relaxation in it.

> "Knowledge without practice is like a glossy fruit. In the same way, practice without our heart is like the illumination of a glow worm."

Practising with complete involvement means strategically weaving the clothes of the present with the threads of heart. That means we are offering ourselves to the task at hand. It is similar to how a tailor stitches a dress that perfectly matches our measurements.

There are no ups and downs when it comes to practicing something.

Whether it is the work of a blacksmith or a potter, what is important is learning the technique to do it well.

Whether it is a pearl shell or the snowflakes on grass, the rays of the Sun touch them the same way. When you do anything lovingly, there is no room for discrimination.

It is crucial to have the right guru for good practice.

A guru works like a lamp to show the right track.

The most notable artists, sportsmen, scholars, politicians of the world also have gurus.

To learn something, one should have a 'Child's Curiosity'. Children usually listen with open minds whenever a new thing is told. Their minds are always on the process. They keenly observe the techniques. They don't think about the outcome.

We often hear from parents —

'My 5-year-old learnt skating so easily. Though I tried many times, I couldn't learn it.';

'My daughter was able to learn French within 30 days.'

This is because children's minds are always in the present, unlike us who spend most of our time either in the past or the future. While watching television, we are so engrossed in it but not otherwise.

A dear friend for practice is 'habit'.

It is vital to be aware of our habits. We can form new habits and let go of unfavourable ones with awareness. In this way, we don't have to be enslaved to our habits and can live a life of freedom.

According to a study, it may become a habit if you do a task continuously for 21 days. Following this technique, we can form new habits and get rid of old ones. If we treat every habit as a process and watch it like a bystander, we can achieve the needed change. Here, don't think of a habit as a weakness or an emotional urge. It is also a practice.

A lot of folks think that practice means labour. In practice, the effort flows like blood through its veins. It is not the same as labour. Also, don't mistake practice as some curse or fate.

When a heart lends its hand to an effort called Warm milk, practice comes out like a thick curd. A meal cooked with love is always delicious. To The same meal, when devotion is added, it Becomes an offering or 'prasadam'.

In the same way, what are we adding to our effort? Our soul? Our mind? Or our body?

Do the methods of practice create creativity? Or kill creativity?

To answer this question and understand it well, we need to delve into the depths of creativity or imagination.

Is creativity a gem that blossoms from the mud? Or is it an elixir that showers from the heavens?

People say that unless one accumulates a massive credit score in previous births, one isn't born a Lata Mangeshkar, a Raja Ravi Verma, or a Rabindranath Tagore.

We always tend to relate creativity to remarkable expertise in art. We also think that we don't have creativity in us and dangerously believe that as Cod's gift.

If we are tender-hearted and have faith that every being in this universe has its unique quality, we can all be creative. If you carefully observe, no object is made without creativity. Remember, if we are not creative, it simply means that we have chosen a path that doesn't suit us.

Many of us think it would be awesome to know our destiny upfront. Imagine you knew everything upfront; wouldn't life be bland?

Life is beautiful because of its unpredictability. That's what makes it attractive as we unfold every moment and day like a new gift. Finding ourselves in the ignorance of darkness lies the natural sweetness of life.

Simply reaching the shore on the other side doesn't make a skipper delighted. We are all creative. It is not limited to a few luminaries on stage. Irrespective of our field, we can be creative and joyfully sing like the cuckoo and fly like a bird.

Creativity is not a Profession; It is an Instinct.

If we expect something in the name of creativity, how can it be creative?

Our longing for fame, wealth and lust kills the power of creativity or imagination within us. For those who want them, creativity is but a disguise.

The creative ones may or may not make wealth or fame. Yet, they live like a king without a crown. They don't expect or long for anything. For them, their work is music and, life, a dance.

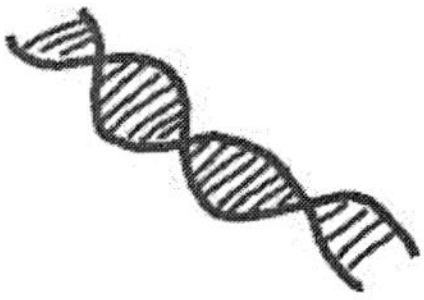

We believe that intelligence is related to one's genes. In 1997, scientists figured out that six chromosomes decide our level of intelligence. Robert J. Plomin conducted extensive research on this subject. It was a practice to measure a child's brilliance in the western world.

What is Intelligence?

Is it a memory? Is it an analytical capability? Is it an imaginative power?

When we add logical thinking to memory, intelligence comes out. The genes related to intelligence don't grow in a vacuum. They need a society and a culture. That is why the learned say that no one becomes wise by birth.

Then, what about geniuses?

They are like the sunflowers in a field of grass chamomiles. The only difference between them and the commoners is their nature rather than capabilities. While the commoners live in the pursuit of luxuries, geniuses live for a cause. The geniuses proffer knowledge to society. However knowledgeable a genius might be, he cannot be born in the air. Just as one can't give birth without the contribution of a male, one cannot become a genius without the influence of society around him.

That is why geniuses are gems born out of the mud but not without the mud.

We can categorise human beings into three types based on intelligence levels.

Those who chew books like goats eat leaves.

Those who chew books and digest a little and, when needed, recollect a little just like cows that bring out a small portion of the gulped food.

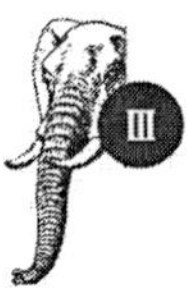
Those who chew the books a little but learn a lot from the surroundings and by nature think deeply on their own like elephants.

In the above three types, the folks in the first category will always spend time reading. They are experts in putting it down as it is.

Memory is the lifeline of their knowledge. Some children by heart the names of countries and capitals, general knowledge questions and answers, and recite the Bhagavad Gita easily. Society calls them experts, scholars, and child prodigies.

The people in this first category study others. But, no one studies them. They get washed away along the stream of time.

Folks in the second category apply the knowledge they gained and add a little of their own to it, just like how we construct more floors in a building.

They add colours and accessories and give it a new look. Or else they create a new thing with the old one as the base for their idea. Society calls them researchers, creative artists, and architects. Such people stand as a reflection of the time we live in.

Folks in the third category think beyond their experiences. Their thoughts are not like the stalks (of a Banyan tree) that hold onto the ground.

Instead, they are the showers of elixir from the skies. Their creativity is a guiding light to the human race at all times, like the North Star. They are timeless. People call them prophets, great philosophers, eminent poets, and artists.

From the contribution point of view, if we look at these three categories of people, we find that the works done by the first category are majorly beneficial to themselves. The works done by the folks belonging to the second category are mutually beneficial to themselves and society. Finally, the works of the third category are valuable to people of all times.

Those who do not belong to the above three categories are the commoners. They live day to day without any concern for knowledge. They run around for food, just like ants surrounding sweet. For them, hunger is the primary urge. Not thought. Their lives are all about dealing with everydaysituations, craving and fulfilling what gives them instant gratification. They only walk in a well-laid path.

Creativity is like an inexhaustible vessel (Akshaya Patra). It will only give more and more as you reap from it. Its sweet fragrance spreads in all directions. It only knows giving but doesn't know to expect anything in return. It doesn't know how to hide at all.

Creativity happens when a birth is supported by nurturing. When one consumes the elixir of practice, one gains knowledge. Notice this. Speaking is natural. But singing is an outcome of practice.

” *Knowledge is what one learns beyond what Nature teaches,' says James Baldwin, an evolutionary scientist.*

Cold that is engraved shines as an ornament.

A complete vessel has no necessity to live.

After writing furiously for about 33 years, Jibson cried out, 'Now, what is left for me?'. Five years from then, he became old and left his body.

After composing 6000 songs, Rabindranath Tagore wept before Cod, saying, 'I haven't yet sung the song that I wanted to sing.'

So, don't go mad about trying to draw that perfect picture. Keep on drawing pictures. Keep on singing songs. A true artist is never complete. He keeps on trying. His effort is an improved version of his earlier one but is never perfect or done for him.

Is creativity natural? Or is it nurtured?

A lot of us think that creativity is that which is different from the current trend. However, mixing colours and painting on the canvas alone is not what creativity means.

The one who got the ability to build a bridge between two unrelated aspects is a genius, says Einstein. The neurons in the brain naturally create new connections in gaining knowledge. With practice, these neurons get more power.

The relation between practice and creativity is like a plant and sunlight. At the beginning of this article, this idea is what Pablo Sarasate candidly expressed based on his life experiences, 'The world called me a genius after I practised fourteen hours a day for 37 years'.

❑

Goals and Means

I came on duty to Sriharikota. I chanced upon Pulicat lake, one of the largest brackish water ecosystems after Chilika lake in Odisha. Here, I saw various migratory birds, which I heard were about two lakhs in number, that travel thousands of miles every year from Siberia to avoid fiery winters. Their sight stunned me for multiple reasons.

I wondered how these birds came from Siberia to Pulicat in Andhra Pradesh, just like how Vasco da Gama discovered the sea route to India. Did they already fix a goal to come here, or did they find Pulicat in the process of finding ways to get out of the scorching winters of Siberia? Whatever the reason, I felt what unexpected hindrances these birds might have endured with resilience across thousands of miles before they finally reached Pulicat.

When we go on the right path, goals will form by themselves. I wonder whether one needs motivational speeches and endless classes to develop goals.

Can one create goals just because we constantly rub them on having them? And can such plans stand the test of time?

I say this because when I force myself to sit and write a poem, I find it impossible to create any decent one. However, I could write with ease when I felt the urge to burst out a deeply felt emotion.

So, what is right?

The path that Niccold Machiavelli chose (political deceit, deviousness, realpolitik) or the path that Mahatma Gandhi walked (truth, non-violence, renunciation, humility, equanimity)?

The way that we choose decides our happiness.

Who doesn't want to be happy? However, the path we choose decides which kind of happiness fades away and which type stays come what may. Some folks say that a good attitude doesn't fit their very nature. But I doubt how many really know their nature. For example, do they mistake their raging desires to be their nature?

Know that everyone and everything has a nature. This includes birds, animals, and Mother Nature too. We often hear that children's nature is very close to Mother Nature's. Who can deny that children are the most loving and happy beings around us?

That is why we hear that there is happiness only when our path is harmonious with Mother Nature. Indeed, that is what our natural approach is. Every environmental summit and debate are about this aspect so that planet Earth can be an excellent place for all.

Does the right path mean 'be good'? Does being good require one to be truthful, kind, and righteous?

Possessing these noble qualities doesn't mean the accumulation of knowledge about them. It means putting them into practice. Isn't it? Let us not assume that good people need not care for anything. In fact, they need to be more cautious.

Life can be compared to that of driving a vehicle. If you are diligent enough, you will reach your destination safely in one piece. Else, you know. This applies to life as well. How can you not agree after seeing so many specimens around!

Whether you are composing a song or living your life, at the end of the day, its beauty lies in the journey and that is what you will cherish for times to come. Won't you? And that is possible only when it is driven by principles. Hence, the path we choose shouldn't be compromised for short term gains because the long term can become irrevocably ugly. The same logic applies to every walk of life. The path or means that we choose decides the quality of our life.

So, how do I recognize that I am on the right path?

The litmus test to this is - 'how do I feel?' This feeling is our CPS. When we are on the right track, we feel confident, assertive, driven and happy. Else, we are fearful, doubtful, bored, and suffer from low self-esteem. Remember, CPS indicates the right direction, and the instant alerts it issues when we deviate. Similarly, our experience works like a yardstick of our performance throughout our path.

When we succumb to greed, anger, jealousy or ego, we can be firmly assured that our journey is in the wrong direction. Hence, I feel that all you have to do is listen to your inner voice that comes from your heart. It will never fail in showing you the right path. In this path, we gain our life experiences, which enlighten us. This enlightenment steers us to the most appropriate route to lead a fearless life.

What role do human values play in this path?

Tell me, what is the value of zero? Indeed, it is 'nothing'. However, mathematics became a possibility only when we believed in that 'zero'. If you add a zero to a number at the right place, it will become something. Or maybe anything. Isn't the sky the limit as you keep adding zeroes to the right place? The same logic applies to human values too. Independently, they make no sense. Yet, when we lead our lives with them, life turns terrific and most valuable.

Some people exhibit values as if they are wearing a wig for society's sake. No doubt, the wig may garner a decent appearance and can aid in forming some opinions about us. Yet, isn't it a burden to carry on this drama in each of our appearances in a society that we have to face every day? Instead, why can't we breathe those values into our lives as naturally as the fragrance of flowers?

Would you agree that one needs to adopt the proper methods to drive well?

Any sensible driver would say a 'yes'.

Whether it is life or driving, the destination is not sufficient. Nor is finding a path to reach that destination enough.

Then what do we require?

Correct methods with proper skills. These are what help us manoeuvre progressively on our path.

One attains finesse not by force or documented guidelines but by open and free imagination to try a less trodden path and create unforeseen things.

You would have noticed almost in every industry how old industries or old ways of doing things have been rapidly disrupted by new ideas or new ways of doing things.

Theatres to OTT platforms, CDs to cloud music, paperbacks to audiobooks, oil to electric vehicles, owning to renting, brick and mortar stores to online stores and many more.

We cannot achieve this finesse simply by walking on an established road. One needs to have open-mindedness. One has to think and act differently. And this quality comes only with imagination.

What is it that imagination cannot do? It has the intrinsic power to create wonders in any field: education, profession, or life.

> — “ ———
> *'WHY ARE WE LIVING' IS THE ‘END’ WHEREAS 'HOW ARE WE LIVING' IS THE ‘MEANS’. THIS ‘MEANS’ IS WHAT WE TERM AS OUR WAY OF LIVING.*
> ——— ” —

The beauty of life lies in our priorities. Our actions change depending on the opportunities and our thoughts. So, likewise, our priorities too change with time.

Having said that, one should be clear with the preferences. These priorities can make or break our life. They have the power to spoil or shine our lives based on our choices. Thus, prioritise according to the path you are in.

So, how does this prioritisation work? How do I prioritise?

We are here again with another simple litmus test. Whatever work is born for you, as you feel, will be yours. That specific work also sends you signals. You will receive it if you are tuned correctly, like the antenna. If you are smart enough, you will embrace it. Secondly, whichever work gives you immense happiness, know that it is yours then and there.

More often, we downplay the power of prioritization. So, in reality, we don't put our hearts on while making choices. Remember, it is the prioritization that introduces us to the world of opportunities. It can drown us in the deep sea if we handle it carelessly.

If we accept that we are the painters of our life, isn't it crucial to choose our colours wisely and paint our dream masterpiece into being?

Is desire a goal?

Desire is attached to the future. Therefore, if we expect something, it will generate desire. This generation of desire is what leads us to form a goal. Thus, we strive to achieve it. In that way, desire creates fuel for action.

Then what is greed? Is it any different from desire?

Creed is like a shadow. Despite your best efforts, you can't hold on to it. Let us understand it this way. For many, luxury and status have become a top priority. I am sure you would have noticed. And some people rub goals onto themselves artificially, as a matter of status symbol. As a result, life is a helpless responsibility for them, for they feel worthless if they don't achieve these goals.

In this case, how can I call these desires strictly? Can I call it greed instead?

Desire is essential, whereas greed is detrimental.

How do I measure desire?

When the desire is big, the risk of achieving it is also equally big. For example, to climb Mount Everest, we have to bear the risk equivalent to its height. If that was a hill, the risk is comparable to that of a hill. Now, what if we don't want to climb at all. Obviously, there will be no risk.

The person ready to take risks can be likened to a flower. Flowers blossom. They face the risk of wind. They withstand the rain. Despite all, they still smile and spread their fragrance. Yet, we see lakhs of people opting to remain as seeds only. Why?

What will happen if we don't have goals? Will such a life be as bad as a boat without any direction?

By the way, what is a goal? Do we require one? Also, is the goal applicable for life or for a task?

Fixing a goal for life means truly caging a pigeon. Life is meant for living. It cannot stop at a goal. It constantly flows. Set a goal for the task. Then life moves. Set new goals for new tasks. It is like this - How much we want to earn is the aim/goal; how we make it is the path.

The end of a journey means the start of another one.

We have to earn our living. If that earning results from our sweat, we will lead a happy life. If it is through stealing others' effort, we have to lead a fearful life. Some are indeed living for money only. Day in and day out, such people are busy counting notes and comparing their stacks with others'. They don't stop at that. They arduously argue that money does wonders.

In my experience, I call these wonders as purposes. One, to provide us comforts. Two, to give us strength. On the flip side, if we make money synonymous with our living, we lose both. If I have to say this bitterly, this is what money can do to us. If we hand over the key of our home to money, it has the power to drag us onto the streets.

Devotion is the path, whereas the Divine is the goal.

Which is first? Devotion or Divine? Is devotion not possible without presuming a form?

I heard that Cod is omnipresent and that if we have devotion, we can see Him anywhere. However, if we develop devotion to reach Cod, can we reach Him? Is that even devotion?

Devotion is meaningless if it has a set intent.

What is the role of the ego in this path?

The ego works like an obstacle in our path. It's like darkness. Even though it doesn't exist, it shows its domination. Only with awareness can we remove darkness with the onset of light. It's futile to fight with ego, for if we have to drive away from the darkness of life, it is possible with light only.

Truth is like a mirror. It will show us our image. So everybody should move ahead, looking into the mirror.

The pressure of aim or goal should not affect our path. We should be involved in the work we do. Work is our path. We should derive happiness from it. With that happiness, we get peace. Of course, we may slip in the journey. Yet, we need to rise and advance our steps. So, what if some mistakes happen. Let's just correct them and proceed further. Remember, it is stupid to imitate others in fear of failure. It is essential to be our natural self.

What stops us from being close to our nature and to mother Nature?

In history, has any effort gone in vain when people stuck to their nature? Not at all.

Will work start with the decision to work? Usually, we decide first to work or not to work. Then we get into that decision. Isn't it? Can't we work without that decision?

When we accept a decision, it amounts to accepting our experience. That experience may be ours or others. This is what knowledge is all about.

Is this knowledge hindrance to the path of truth?

Truth is like an ocean. As we explore more and more, we find more gems. It is rejuvenating all the time. However, the sea is not entirely rosy with treasures and fish. It also has whirlpools and cyclones, to name a few. This indicates that whoever deviates from the path will face tornadoes.

I am sure most of us get influenced either by someone or something. It doesn't matter whether this influence is intentional or unintentional. Let us understand that all our paths and goals result from this influence only. Do you agree? If you agree, you might wonder if we can have a path of our own and make decisions and work without this influence. Hmmm... I must say, not wholly. We won't be totally submerged in this influence. First, however, we have to be aware of its presence.

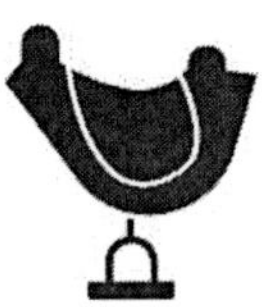

When life is like a horse, these influences should be like saddles that facilitate us to sit on it and ride comfortably rather than blinkers that prevent us from seeing sideways and behind.

Attention is the oxygen of work. When the mind works with full attention, it should not deviate to presumptions. Guesses and presumptions are the enemies of attention. Accept things as they are. And move on. Where there is attention, that is where the present is.

Know that aspiration is also a goal. It may be materialistic or spiritualistic. But, nevertheless, its aim is evidently achievement. Right?

Why do we fix goals?

For satisfaction? For status?

We chase our goals till we are satisfied. However, I am asking you, do we get satisfaction in this pursuit? Unfortunately, many are in the delusion that satisfaction comes with results. That's why they move from one result to another and strive for success.

Can success become a goal?

What would life be if we stopped at one success? It is not possible. Right? Life won't stop at any success. It moves on. It flows. There is no full stop for life, only commas. The goal is artificial. Life is natural.

What is the goal of a child? The child knows no work. Anything is only fun. To those involved in work, where is the need for a goal?

We come across hotels and sarais on our journey. We stop there and rest for a while and then move on. Achievements in life are also like these sarais and hotels.

Socrates, Shakespeare, M.S. Subbalakshmi, Picasso... do they have goals for life? With what goals have they painted their lives so beautifully? Writing is the lifeline of Shakespeare. Singing is the soul of Subbalakshmi. Results come and go. The light of their journey illuminates the globe.

Don't be confused about your goals to the luxuries and comforts around you. Don't create goals in peer pressure. It will only burden you, not lighten you. In the mad rush to match somebody else's desires, you don't have to enslave yourself. That is somebody else's life, not yours.

Everything has evolved, which wasn't seen or dreamt of earlier. Only those with open eyes and a loose personality can adapt and skilfully manoeuvre through life changes with acceptance. Rest will either perish or sulk. That is why I think it is foolish to have a goal that is not beneficial to the overall well-being of the planet. On the other hand, it is equally silly to have an adamant approach (path/means), especially in our fast-paced world.

Remember, your goals should be about what you genuinely care for, not what others rub onto you. Let us again relook at driving. To drive well, one needs the right skillset. Having a goal to drive is not good enough if one doesn't develop the necessary skills and acquire the finesse over time.

The goal is like a mirage in the desert of life.
The path is like an oasis.

Every second. Mother Nature handles every disruption and changes happening to itself. So should be our life too.

When you are adaptable and involved totally, the destination ought to happen. It is like this. If you eat nutritious food, exercise and rest well regularly, good health is bound to happen. Health cannot be your goal. It is a consequence of the path you chose.

When it comes to means or path - Doing what you don't like is the path of the fools and cowards; Doing what you like is the path of the intelligent and resilient; Doing what is needed is the wise' path.

When you are entirely involved in whatever you do, you don't need to create goals; they will just happen. Your involvement will only make you more competent, resilient and effective in everything you do.

Remember, a goal is not always meant to be reached; it often serves simply as something to aim at. Flexibility and adaptability are the keys to achieving anything.

❑

Reward and Punishment

For centuries, punishments and rewards have guided humanity like a controlling power. From birth till death, we fluctuate between these two. We have conveniently tagged punishment to unacceptable or bad behaviour and rewarded as acceptable or good behaviour.

Both reward and punishment follow good and bad like a shadow. As the good is aware of the bad, the bad is cognizant of the good. They are not only causatives but complementarians too.

Tell me, would good and bad lose their identity or existence without punishment and reward? Are we behaving well out of fear or desire? How would we be if there were no desire and fear? Have you ever thought about this?

Are all those so-called good people carrying the weight of goodness as a piece of inconvenient baggage? Is goodness our ornamentation, or is it our responsibility?

Have all who promote themselves as good people unconsciously sheltered ego and pride that they are good people as they think they never harmed anyone?

When things don't go as desired, have you observed how the bad inside mocks you and your goodness? At such times, we realize the weight of our goodness. Hence, the lesser you declare about yourself, the lighter you will be.

The conscious effort to become good is indeed taxing. People looking for temporary relief from punishment usually veer towards being good. However, that doesn't mean they genuinely want to be that way.

Remember, we don't become good just because we byhearted the code of conduct in our doctrines and scriptures. When we get trapped in the complementariness of life — profit & loss, joy & sorrow, anger & calm, and likes & dislikes, we only become enslaved to the scheme of punishments and rewards.

Are these 'good' and 'bad' relative to people, countries and situations?

Yes, that's what we see and hear. But, if that is so, can we say that they exist without our intervention? Not at all. In our experience, they are not independent because acceptable behaviour in one place is considered unacceptable in another. So, these are mere experiences that we learn over time and constantly recalibrate our behaviour to suit the circumstances around us. A sheer survival instinct, isn't it? Hence, can I say that our reactions are a consequence of our conditioned experiences?

Are these good and bad things universal and eternal?

Yes, to some extent. When we closely observe them, we find that they originate from our experiences. Since human beings are human beings everywhere and anytime, their core values are similar in all places. That's why the teachings of great philosophers like Socrates, Plato, Shakespeare, Tagore, and Mahatma Gandhi are still relevant today. This also means that there is some common good and bad for all human beings at all times.

We tend to repeat what society accepts or rewards and avoid what is looked down upon or punishes us. That means, before we perform any action, we are historically made to think of the consequences upfront. This exactly is the reason why we fear what we fear. As I vented in my first words towards the beginning, what makes a 16-year young student commit suicide for failing an academic exam?

What makes us do what we dislike and are not good at?

Isn't it related to the greedy reward mechanism?

Memory is a storehouse of reward and punishment. We choose one based on our experience. Ask yourself, if there were no bashings and abuses within home or society, would you continue doing what you are doing now?

Did we get these good and bad with birth? Are these genetic?

Since childhood, our parents, school, society, religion, and nation tutor us this way. We learn division from our elders and community. And then, in return, they control us. As a result, our thinking and behaviours become mechanical. That is why most of our actions are reactionary.

We see parents hugging us when we meet their expectations. We also see them scolding us if we perform otherwise. With time, we get tuned in to get the reward of hugging, for instance. The same is the case with schools and society. We get habituated to this reward and try to avoid punishment. We tune our actions and behaviour accordingly.

'Arishadvargas' are the six enemies of the mind, namely lust, anger, greed, delusion, arrogance, and envy. They steal life from our souls. These enemies are born from desire. The more we enjoy pleasure, the more the desire inflames it. The burning desire will take us on the wrong route. Desire can't be suppressed but can be tamed with detachment. And detachment is possible with discernment.

Are reward and punishment a stimulus?

There are two types of stimuli, i.e., internal and external. The fame, pain, insult, love etc., are internal. The medals, bonuses, cash rewards, promotions, facilities etc., are external. Both these stimuli form part of reward and punishment. Rewards and punishments are positive and negative stimuli, respectively.

Is hunger, pain, insult, money, praise, fame, and power our true motivators?

Will we lead a fulfilling and satisfying life only by refuelling our ego with rewards and avoiding punishment?

Do rewards contribute to better performance?

Psychologists have divergent opinions on this. However, the majority agree that the rewards enhance thirst for more rewards. Motivation should be natural, not induced. Encouragement and guidance will enhance performance. The reward should be an encouragement, rather than a favour.

The spirit behind punishment is to remove unwanted behaviour or to reduce it. By reducing the negative things, it will automatically increase the positive ones. But there is a danger of using punishments frequently. They may develop anger, revenge, and violent behaviour. The punishments should not be tools in the hands of power. Punishment should be commensurate with unwanted behaviour.

The system of rewards and punishment should not be used as a dose of daily nutrition. Instead, we should use it sparingly. Otherwise, life will be a set of automated continuous compulsive reactions.

Where is freedom in compulsion?

Should an artist paint only when there is a reward? Should parents nurture their children in fear of being insulted by society?

Should a student learn only for a hefty paycheck and the comforts of an airconditioned room? Think.

Is ambition or purpose necessary?

Life is evergreen with an aim. It fuels energy to work. When this energy is constant, it becomes a commitment that will become the light of internal stimulus.

> *The pleasures are hungry tigers.*
> *Ambition should not fall prey to it.*

Heaven and hell are a form of reward and punishment. We believe that good will be rewarded with heaven, and the bad will be punished in hell.

Are men virtuous because of Cods and heaven? If they knew that there are no Cods and heavens, would they leave their virtues?

If the fear of hell is genuine, there shouldn't be any sinner. Isn't it? The centre of virtue or sin is the mind. First, we commit mistakes there and also get punished there itself. Our inner voice is the real motivator. Listen carefully.

The system of rewards and punishments is prevalent in schools. Teachers reward their students in different forms. They believe that these rewards will encourage students for better results. The famous psychologist Thorn Dike also supports this view. At the same time, the teachers use punishment as a deterrence.

This system will kill the natural intuition to learn most of the time. The real motivation for learning is to create an atmosphere and culture for learning.

Many parents don't respect their children's ideas. They dictate decisions and enforce them. They try to get their wishes fulfilled through their children. They don't care about their children's minds.

What do the children want from their parents?

Rewards? No.

No. They want time. They want love at that time. Nothing else. No career discussion, no progress cards, no medals.

Will high pay, bonuses, and perks attract talent? Yes, of course.

Will a company sustain its talent longer with financial benefits? No.

What's the way then? Transparency and impartiality combined with a progressive career will be a better answer. The ethos of a company will make it.

What is Reinforcement Theory?

Skinner says that we can reinforce the same behaviour with a stimulus. He added reinforcement to the Thorn Dyke theory of law of effect. He says that the same behaviour repeats and strengthens with rewards.

These theories are definite that the external stimulus will influence the internal one. However, these theories have limitations. The demand ends with reward or punishment. When our demands get fulfilled, we reward. We punish if it is otherwise.

Demand doesn't give freedom to others. If we replace demand with the request, it allows us to exercise our minds. In request, we lose interest in reward and punishment.

Role of Discipline in Reward & Punishment Scheme

Rewards and punishments play a crucial role in relationships also. The reward and punishment system works on the principle of discipline. Discipline is based on subordination. Subordination is enforced through discipline.

From family to the nation, every institution finds a mechanism of discipline. Whether it may be self-discipline or external discipline, the principle enforces specific rules and regulations over the individual. Rewards and punishments are aids in this enforcement.

Resistance is the natural response to discipline. The individual adjusts himself to the institution. To avoid unpleasant feelings of punishment, the individual adopts the standard code. Either it may be ethics, morals or laws. When the discipline crosses its limits, resistance comes to the streets. The authority tries to suppress it. If it couldn't, then it compromises.

Both resistance and compromise are axles between individuals and authority. As long as there is a balance, the system runs smoothly. Rewards and punishments should not make the man dependent. It should shape his selfreliance.

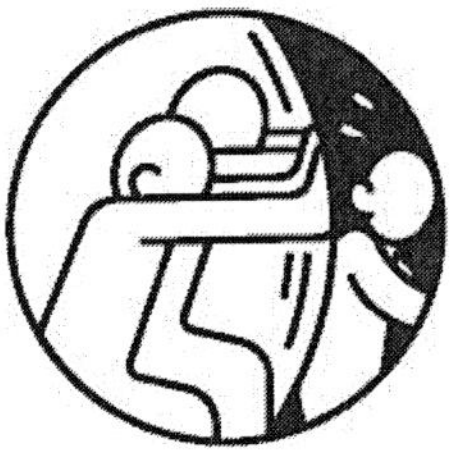

Rejection is also a form of punishment. Man tries to change his behaviour or actions when they are rejected by others. Those people who are involved in work that is unacceptable to society will be seen by society with rejection. That is why everyone wants to get acceptance of their actions by this society. The same is the case with the governments also.

Man is looking at death as a punishment. Death is a surprise. He wishes to die in a peaceful manner. For that, he indulges in worship and rituals.

Which is better? Reward or Punishment?

On this subject. Harvard University psychologists conducted a test named 'Prisoner's dilemma'. In this game, the people who got awards performed twice as well as those who got punishment. But, at the same time, those who trained well have performed better than the untrained. This is because the mental development of the children who are not physically punished is much better than those who are not.

Then how will it be when there is only the reward without punishment? And there is only good without bad?

It is similar to the expectation that there is only a day without night. Can we live without night?

Khalil Gibran defined 'bad' in his book 'Prophet' as

'Bad is nothing but the good which has suffered from hunger and pain'.

There is no completeness in accepting one and rejecting the other. Duality is the thought of Nature. Therefore, we cannot have peace and happiness in conflict and contradiction.

Reward and punishment are like the two eyes of man. The mind always hovers around awards. It wants to possess it constantly. In that process, it suffers. The mind should not run after the reward to relieve the punishment.

Let us allow life to flow as natural as the stream.

Let us allow it to blossom as beautiful as a flower.

There is no need to impose any targets or thoughts artificially. It will be a magnificent gift to work and travel with the journey as the goal.

❑

Aspirations and Opportunities

"We should use our things and love our people," said the wise. However, we are using people and loving things.

Businesses worldwide compete to attract and fulfil human desires or aspirations. Marketing and advertising expenditures have gone sky-high, showcasing countless varieties. They entice us with attractive messages, captivating colours, and high-quality products. We have numerous models, from a small pin to a pen and a clock to a car, creating curiosity. There is a comprehensive display of branded clothes, graded footwear, irresistible fashions, and designs.

How many times have we gone to a store for something and ended up buying another or more? Many times. Right? Yet, we see our happiness dipping in no time when we come across a new model released in the market, be it an expensive cell phone, a luxury car or a flashy home. The one who could afford branded wear loses heart when he finds his friends wearing another appealing one. A vehicle purchased is going outdated in less than two years. Everyone changes their mobile phones.

from a tongawala to a business magnate. Even with a new phone in our hands, our eyes are always on the gadget in another's hands.

Finally. I have an open question to ask.

Are our aspirations creating things? And are worldly things driving us?

Why do we love things? What are we aspiring to achieve from them? Is there a meaningful gain in possessing them?

We all want permanent happiness, and our journey is in seeking it. Our mind shows us various paths. One of these paths is this world of things.

The mind deludes us to believe that there is happiness in things. Once we possess that thing, the mind shows us another thing. Once one desire fulfils, a new desire crops upon seeing another thing. This is how our life moves on from one desire to another. It passes away in our endless hunt for items. There is no rest for this hunting.

One after the other, we keep refuelling desires. If we achieve it, we enjoy the momentary pleasure it gives. And if we don't achieve it, we become unhappy. Fulfilled passions ignite vanity in us while unfulfilled ones do the opposite. In this way, we spend our lives wavering between the struggles of hopes and disappointments.

The human mind is a bundle of desires. There is nothing that it doesn't want. It keeps on asking for more and more as we fulfil each of them. It wants you to accomplish everything that it desires. It's a toxic circle. In this circle, a thing stems from a desire and a desire stems from a thing.

Desires induce the senses, and the senses find pleasure in them. We should not mistake such a pleasure for happiness. Remember that it is not permanent and aids as nutrition for desires.

> *The man who longs for constant pleasure clings onto the hook of desire.*
>
> *He misses life.*
> *He presumes pleasures as life.*

Another powerful deception in the toxic circle of desires and things is in the name of 'choice' or 'selection'. The connection between numerous things and desires is 'choice'. Our senses pick one item from many things, just as a gambler chooses a card from a pack. Although this choice gives pleasure, it also includes some future concerns.

Nowadays, it has become an arduous task for parents in deciding on a school for their children. Irrespective of the school, it concerns them that it needs to fulfil their desires.

Their children have to become doctors, engineers, or collectors. Some parents want their children to imbibe business acumen and skills. So, they accordingly choose a school that can fulfil their desire after 20 years. When they meet parents with a similar disposition and suggest another school, they doubt their selection and get disappointed. In no time, they again begin their search for a better school. As a result, doubts arise in both the parents and their children.

Having said that, alternatives increase the creative aspect in individuals. They will find the right thing in the market that matches their likes. They think of a better product than the one they are using. This thought gives birth to another product. Our nature is the reason for our different and distinct desires.

According to the differences in societal and economic aspects, our desires and resultant pleasures occur. For instance, there is a vast difference between the desires of forest dwellers and urbanites.

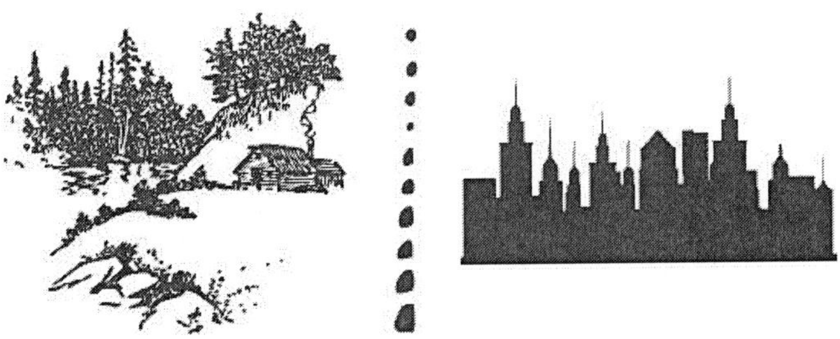

In the same manner, the desires of the Americans differ from those of the Africans. There is a difference in the desires even among people who live in the same area. This condition applies to even members of the family living under the same roof. Varied choices are what lead to options in the world of things.

Alternatives are an indication of progress.

Primitive man had limited options. Since he was dependent on the resources available in the forest, his desires were also limited to what was available around him.

When things don't fulfil one's desires, it will encourage new thoughts. These new thoughts once again lead to the invention of new products. Although these products give temporary pleasure, they also enhance new ideas.

Imagination takes man towards advancement. If there is no diversity in things, it will slow down our thoughts. Dead desires don't create new things. When there is diversity, there will be a possibility for progress. It creates enthusiasm to work with vigour.

Cravings are like mirages. They give the satisfaction of being fulfilled but don't. They only make you feel that you are contented. But in reality, you aren't.

The varieties in things make one think we are deriving immense pleasure. It is like the senses getting comfort on a soft bed. However, the very next moment, there is dissatisfaction. And immediately arises a new desire, craving for the variety, and the race for a new product.

The feeling of lacking will disturb the body and mind. This is because we oscillate between light and shadow of the complementariness of life, i.e., pleasures and pains.

We all want to come out of dissatisfaction. But, how? Can we attain contentment within the realm of things? No. It is like applying a pain balm for a heart attack. Again, a severe pain.

What about if we suppress dissatisfaction? It bounces like a coiled spring. Dissatisfaction leads to sorrow. Dissatisfaction leads to disappointment.

What is the reason for our dissatisfaction? A thing? Or a desire?

The dominion of things is the foundation for our aspirations.

Is desire first? Or thing?

If there were no things, won't there be a desire?

Desires are there to be fulfilled. Else dissatisfaction burns us. To achieve, one needs to have something.

If we have only one thing, we get bored. So, we have various items to address different desires. From the bundle of alternatives, our passion gets to choose one thing. If we get pleasure out of fulfilment, we tend to get more from the same thing. Here, the law of diminishing returns works. When the pleasure starts depleting, we start looking for alternatives.

Why did pleasure weaken?

The fulfilled desire starts comparing with that of the neighbour. There is room for jealousy, insecurity, and anxiety as long as there is comparison.

For instance, we join our child in various schools after evaluating the multiple boards like SSE, CBSE, and ICSE. However, when another school shows promising results compared to our child's school, we feel sad. Similarly, we buy a car after doing extensive research. However, the moment a new model appears in the market, we lose interest in our vehicle. In this way, how long do we run after desires and choices? We should stop.

To stop, we are chaining our desires and increasing our attention on what we have. We are cutting the wings of our desires. By detaching ourselves from the glittery choices, we find relaxation. Instead of jumping like a frog towards choices, we habituate ourselves to stay steady like the tortoise. We are increasing our love for our home, family, air. and land. We have inherited customs, traditions, religions, castes, values, and joy & sorrows from society. We have choices in these as well. Yet, we all love only those that don't enforce us. This detachment is not what is necessarily rubbed by external forces.

Because of the experiences since childhood, the people who influence us, we formulate a particular way of living. This happens naturally. Our food habits, customs, & traditions, rules and regulations have evolved over a while. These changes happened because of the surroundings of our birth, upbringing, and introspection.

Although the market provides thousands of varieties, we would take what's necessary. Similarly, punctuality, good behaviour, gentleness, desire for peace, honesty, and effort are the good dictums we created for ourselves over time.

In a way, discipline is a consequence of these good dictums. In searching for solutions, we are losing our inner beauty. In reality, answers to our doubts lie within us only. Therefore, we need to observe the signals our inner voice sends. If we look deep inside, it will be evident. Like a compass, it will direct us in the right direction. In this direction, there is clarity. In that clarity, there is an answer. In that answer, there is relaxation. That relaxation brings peace and happiness.

When a man wants to attain peace, and when he wants to save himself from the choices, he has to lead life by principles.

Most of us are interested in only the outcome in the current turbulent atmosphere. We somehow want to attain the fruit of it. Whatever be the way, we are interested in our destination. If one wants to reach the goal and doesn't want to give importance to the course, it is as good as ignoring all principles. There is no scope for fluctuations if we lead our lives based on truthfulness, honesty, simplicity, kindness, plain-heartedness, and righteousness. If we can stand amidst the difficulties, we can stay committed and courageous.

Remember, there will be a test every day in the above-mentioned principled life. Every day we will see the outcome. We get to assess our every movement and move forward. Such a life will not worry about the results. It believes that the result is a natural outcome of the path. If the journey is good, the results will be good. There should be clarity in the chosen path. That path should come from within.

Are we responsible for the creation of desire? Can't we separate ourselves from our desires? If we can't, why has it become the problem? Why do we wish to destroy it? Even wanting to destroy it is also a desire. Isn't it?

We categorise desires as happy, sorrowful, good, and bad ones. We are encouraging the good ones and rejecting the bad ones. The real problem is in competing with desires and fighting with them. We should not categorise or resist them. We alone can find the answer to our situation when we observe this basic desire. Then, with the understanding of the desire in its complete form, we get happiness.

Despite having many, man always longs for something more. The thirst to have this and that always haunts a man. In this haunting, he loses his sense and common sense. Without this knowledge, man gets trapped in this vicious circle. In addition to the struggle between the joys and sorrows of desires, we struggle with the turbulence of this duality.

So, how do we quench this thirst?

Every attempt to quench this thirst will only further increase it. That is why it is essential to teach the mind contentment. We should adopt simplicity in our lifestyle. Contentment gives us happiness and steadiness. Such a steady mind alone can travel towards knowledge.

In that knowledge, our rational mind will take us away from 'Use people and love things' to 'Use things and love people'.

In this path, we use what is necessary - using water for our necessities, and bringing to our experience the joy of being welcomed by the flowers that sway contented after absorbing the needed sunlight.

❑

Mother Tongue

Here is a small event that I came across as a visiting officer to a remote village. The village has a government school and a private school. We all noticed how the government schools gradually got washed away in the deluge of private schools. One day, I happened to attend the private school's annual function as their chief guest. All the children lined up to wish me warmly 'Good Morning'. I blushed at their innocence and gently asked them what 'Good Morning' meant. They couldn't answer. Then I marched into their inside corridors where some of them greeted me with a 'Welcome Sir' for which they had no clue about again. In short, this minor incident shows the current state of affairs. Here below, let us methodologically see why it is so.

The number of children studying in English medium schools has been exponentially rising in our country. For instance, in Bihar alone, this number grew to 47 times between 2008 and 2014, while a meagre number joined the Hindi medium schools. When it comes to the southern states of India, this number is even more alarming.

With the advent of liberalization/globalization policies, a vast majority of the government schools shut their doors. They found their excuses and justified why the English medium had a superior advantage over local languages in the current market economy. As a result, we have seen that nearly one-fourth of our children study in English medium schools over a while.

And not just that, we are proudly publicizing all over that we are a treasure-chest of English-speaking people to grab the much-needed employment opportunities. As per American population statistics, America had nearly 17 lakh migrated Indians in 2000. This number grew close to 28.5 lakhs in 2010.

The Sun rises in the east. But it is indifferent and impartial to every being in the east. We can notice that the areas in the west are relatively developed in comparison to their eastern counterparts. It may be a district, a state, a country, or a globe ...we can find this observation in general. As a result, the people in the east are migrating to the west. They have to learn foreign languages. Almost ten lakh people migrate to America every year, clearly showing the mounting pressure to learn English.

Today, no place is an island because of globalization. Across the world, lakhs and lakhs of people migrate to developed countries for better living conditions and job opportunities. As a result, standardization has become the new market mantra that resulted in a total wipe-out of umpteen languages. For instance, in the 17th century, Canada had approximately sixty actively spoken languages. However, today, it has only one that is actively used. At this rate, the world will lose more than half of the seven thousand currently prevailing languages or dialects.

Languages are the primary means of keeping our culture alive and connected to one's history, and roots.

What is a mother tongue? Is it simply the language that your mother speaks?

No. It is much beyond mere words. The voice of the land, the waters, the fauna, the flora, and everything that grows within its tender shelter keeps one connected to it emotionally. It is no different from the two doting mothers. Nature and our mother. There is so much warmth in our language. But we are all craving worldly benefits and have started taking diktats in English.

Despite our success outside, most of us are still in search of inner happiness. Why? Mother tongue is a relationship that develops gradually with one's land. It means that we draw our emotional strength from our soil. We will struggle internally in our unconscious slavery to alien forces because our core is built with the essence of the homeland's fragrance. That is why people find no contentment despite immense prosperity visible on the exterior. This observation clearly shows that creating an atmosphere suitable to one's roots is essential to see a gratifying outcome.

One's conscience suffers from remorse when one alienates from the known to replace it with the unknown. This sense of guilt grows like cancer gradually. If I were to look for a resemblance, mother tongue is like mother's milk. A child fed with it naturally finds it easy to digest anything and has higher immunity in fighting unforeseeable diseases. Similarly, children who are strong in their mother tongue can quickly grasp other languages and make a mark for themselves comfortably in the world.

Fortunately, research proved that it is easier to learn a new language when a person knows their mother language well. Even if we go by scientific study, assimilation of information, personality, and intellectual development were the highest in people whose education was in their mother tongue.

Moreover, in 2002, the United Nations openly announced a clear correlation between mother tongue and one's overall well-being.

In 2008, UNESCO declared that children taught in their mother tongues are way smarter mentally and emotionally than those taught in a foreign medium.

Often, the direct translation of one language into another can never convey the same essence and feel as that of the the source language. The scholars and authors of the world will vouch for this fact. Therefore, the best way to know a culture or its people thoroughly is to understand the language of the land.

Knowing the language of the land not only enhances our self-esteem, but it also enriches our confidence and creates awareness of why we are the way we are.

Without understanding who we are and our values, what meaningful progress can we make in society?

Which society will respect one who has no clue of one's identity?

How can we become strangers like guests or tourists to our motherland?

Here is good news for those of us who believe that happiness is in making more money. Businesses are going the local way, so the importance of mother tongues has increased exponentially.

If you want to become an entrepreneur, knowing your mother tongue to communicate with your local customers has become beneficial. The possibilities of making money with the help of one's mother language are enormous in today's economy.

We are all chasing success, competing with everyone to achieve something, and fighting within ourselves to occupy the golden throne. Simultaneously, we are losing our hearts and minds in this race for success. Ironically, we are receiving sorrow along with the crown.

Every individual wishes to lead a life without any sorrows. However, we are unable to imagine a life without competition. We are foolishly searching for happiness in comparisons and competitions, just like an idiot who endlessly looks into the skies for the Moon on a New Moon Day.

We are deeply ingrained that life is worthless without goals, aspirations, and competitions. That is why our children are constantly haunted by the pressure to win.

An education that strips away one's self-respect is like a glossy fruit. But, tell me, how can there be a place for self-respect in a society that treats its mother tongue as an orphan and a fugitive? How can the soul express itself in an education system treading on an axle of imitation?

Whether children or adults, we are all scared of exams in our respective academic and career pursuits. Instead of considering exams as part of our learning experience, we see them as the elixir to fulfil our aspirations. As a result, children are unable to face even minor obstacles. They do not have the strength to face difficulties.

Cone are the times when one was ready to go against the stream. Today's children are unable to go even along with the stream. Language has the unique capability to tame the fire within. It is well equipped to share the burden of our thoughts, behaviour, customs and motive. If such a language flows from the mind than from the heart, what else can we expect but fear in our children during exams?

Children are like the rays of the Sun. They should bathe themselves entirely in the self-knowledge of sunlight. But, instead, they are mugging up words within the four walls that are illuminated with electricity.

Every creature in this world calls its near and dear in its unfeigned language. How are we different?

How can a language emerge from a cold, emotionless and restrained atmosphere?

Aren't we sacrificing our imaginations for a little bitty stomach?

Ask yourself whether it is the jobs and packages that are deciding the language we speak.

Are we living with self-respect and pride? Is it not that the memory is riding over creativity?

Did we realize that we have unknowingly prioritized memory over creative abilities?

Did we know that we compromised our peace of mind for the enormous treasure of wealth that has no imagination, creation, and creativity in life?

Mother tongue is the language that we hear and grow with. Such a language can give a definite shape to our feelings and thoughts. Who can deny that it is convenient to converse in our language? Also, tell me, aren't you happy expressing your deeply felt emotions, be it joy or sorrow, in your language? Of course, you do.

A body that cannot emanate emotions is like a stringless guitar. Fascinated by Mother Nature, children should sound like alluring music. As new thoughts adorn them like clothes, they should gleefully sing immersed. In the trees of their bodies, birds should sing like new ideas. In such an atmosphere, we can find gems emerging even amidst rocks.

One should ideally take an individual from the known to the unknown. However, we are being driven from the unknown to an even bigger unknown in the current educational system.

Aren't we coercing our tender minds with an unfamiliar language and making ourselves a stranger to our known language?

Imagine if you have to enter your own house like a relative. What would that feel like?

And what about the subconscious dilemma we all face in the classrooms when we don't come across any of those things that we heard or imagined as we grew up?

Isn't this creating an unbelievable distance between us and our experiences? Aren't we trying hard to fit into others' experiences?

Suppose language is a barrier to one's feelings. Why don't we create a device that removes this obstacle by facilitating the free flow of one's language?

We need a gadget that translates our feelings into another person's language. Here, it is not just about hearing; it should facilitate visuals too.

With the help of the gadget, one should be able to read content in their mother tongue, which was written in a foreign language. This should not be a device for the selected few. It should get into the mainstream so that everyone has access to it. We should ensure that the device doesn't compromise emotions. The choice of words should be simple for any layman to follow. This should aid during our conversations with foreigners and in our audio or written exams given in a foreign language. The gadget should remove the gap between the speaker and the listener, between the subject and the student.

For instance, if a Japanese talks to us, we should hear it in our mother tongue. Similarly, the Japanese should listen in their mother tongue when talking in ours.

When there is no difference between what we speak and what we study, our hearts will bloom and spread fragrance around. Would we study in English or any foreign medium if such a device is mentioned above? I don't think so.

Let us realize that we are all hanging onto English for survival or hunger's sake. But, can we leave the sweetness of our mother tongue?

Hasn't the technological revolution bowed to the development of the Chinese, Japanese and the Russians in their mother-tongues?

If this digital revolution can get such a gadget, we will all lovingly hug our mother tongue. Won't we? Be it eating, drinking, thinking, and enjoying, we will all be doing it in our mother tongue only. So, while the language gadget takes care of our career, our hearts can care for our instincts or predispositions.

When nature adorns itself in diversity, why are we adorning ourselves stealthily?

We have invented the uniform to cover the gaps between our economic classes. But we are being crushed by rollers by the same educational system that disregards our likes and dislikes and uniqueness. We limit ourselves to studying sciences and English instruction mediums just as we raise chickens in poultry farms.

Every parent wants a Satya Nadella or a Sundar Pichai in his home. If this is not aspirational eugenics, then what can we call this? If science could produce a thousand Einsteins with gene mutation, can you imagine what this world would look like?

Let us provide a fertile land where every plant can grow. Let us create a conducive atmosphere. Let us build our schools that respect the nature and instincts of our children. Children should get the opportunity to study their choices rather than compulsions. We should have experts to guide our children for each of these options. Teachers should not be mandated to teach all subjects.

Our educational system should be based on our children's nature and interests, right from primary education to doctorate. In the government schools, some schools should be designated to handle only arts & sciences, some for sports, some for immediate job market needs, and some for research.

THE EDUCATION WHICH ALIENATES LEARNING FROM THE LAND MAKES A MAN DISCONNECTED AND EMOTIONLESS LIKE A ROBOT.

Remember, we will have all kinds of opportunities to work in the future. If we can focus and concentrate on our work, why will there be an unemployment problem? The education which alienates learning from working makes the man an animal. If the governments could formulate policies with their citizens as the focal point, we would definitely create a happy world. Citizen as the focal point doesn't mean providing food, clothing and shelter. These will turn them into beggars. Instead, government policies should focus on citizens' strengths and capabilities that boost their self-respect. That is where true nation-building begins.

At the end of my talk in the school, I said, "we are killing thousands of Cods with our education. We are creating a gulf between them and their nature and mother nature. A language should be a catalyst for their creativity. Education should touch their hearts and sing. These little stars should shine, illuminating the entire world."

I said, "Mother tongue is the language of the heart, not of the tongue".

The whole class clapped with joy. Yes, I am indeed dreaming of a beautiful world in their hands.

❑

Life and Happiness

What is life? I say 'To live is life'.

Immediately, you question me — 'In that case, who are those who don't live?'. Right?

We can count on our fingertips the number of people who truly live. But, then, how about the remaining? The remaining are dying for living and dying while living.

A famous saying by a poet goes like this - 'There is birth when you open your eyes. There is death when you close your eyes. Life is what happens in the blink of an eyelid.'

How many tides we see, how many surges we face, how many cyclones we go through in this tiny blink! Some will survive. Some will struggle to survive. Some will succumb to struggle. Few will enjoy it as an opportunity. Although we are born to live, what makes us feel sorry about ourselves and believe death is a much easier option?

So, how should one live?

Life should be lived as light as the cotton pins that float effortlessly in the wind. Life should not be a burden. The

very thought - 'Everything is happening because of me' is the base of this burden. 'What will happen to their lives if I am not there. I am doing all of this.' The three rocks 'I, my mine' are components of this burden on our mind suffocating us.

Who am I? I am Arjun; I am an officer; I am a doctor;
I am a businessman; I am a leader.

Who am I? I am a Hindu: I am a Christian; I am a Muslim;
I am a Brahmin, a Reddy a Yadava.

Who am I? I am a capitalist: I am a communist:
I am an environmentalist.

Who am I? I am an Indian: I am an American:
I am a European.

All the above mentioned are groups. We strive for an identity by becoming one in the group. We try to gain power, positions from the group. We feel that belonging to a group brings security in life. We believe that the group accompanies us in all our right & wrongs, weaknesses, limitations, and joy & sorrow.

When asked, 'who are you?', we try to answer through a name, a position, a designation, a community, a region, or a faith. Interestingly, after our death, none address us by any of these designations. Instead, we are called 'corpses' or 'departed souls'. Where has the T that resorted to the above names and frames all this while gone?

Although the group provides all comforts or amenities.

there is always something that our interior world questions us. Whatever we may have, there is always a feeling of lacking that pains us.

Who Am I?

The thought of 'I am a soul that doesn't expect power, position and wealth'. 'I am happiness beyond weaknesses and fears' is the lifeline to a joyful life.

A boulder called 'my' turns life into a burden. 'My' claims ownership of everything and commands everything to follow it. It starts with the physical body 'my hands', 'my legs' and moves onto 'my children', 'my relatives', and so on. 'My' becomes authoritative with countless things — 'my shirt', 'my pants', 'my house', 'my car', and so on. Finally, 'my' starts to wield its power even on other-worldly things like 'my thoughts', 'my ideology', 'my argument', and 'my faith'. A famous saying aptly connotes the rule that our ego called 'my' follows — 'It holds onto the legs until it reaches but will grasp the hair once it gets there'.

Desire is the source of 'my'. It makes a tireless effort to capture everything it eyes. The moment its endeavour becomes fruitful, the authority called 'mine' joins hands with it. Once the 'my' possesses the authority, it will ensure all its likes and dislikes follow the dot. As time passes, our children, whom we thought belonged to 'my', will grow way beyond our control.

Wealth topples down like a pack of cards. Even our own body, which we always feel as our sole proprietorship, stops cooperation...then we begin to question — 'by the way, what is 'mine' in all this?'

A very few of us strive for true and eternal happiness. Still, many find reasons in things, people, and situations. We work day and night, all our lives, for something that we think is ours and is not ours. We lose our sleep to accumulate things to find happiness in them. We struggle for the so-called 'my' people and expect happiness from them.

Did we ever get a thought on what we have done for the one that is genuinely ours, 'soul'? If yes, then the direction of our life will change completely. There is an incident to reflect upon the idea of baggage we carry with us. A train stopped in a small railway station.

An old lady entered the compartment with luggage on her head. The train started moving. Yet, the old lady didn't put her luggage down. Looking at her, an elderly man advised her to keep her luggage down and enjoy the journey. She replied. Won't my luggage become additional burden to this train if I put it down? That is why I am carrying it.'

Similarly, many of us think of life as a burden. We also believe that we are the only ones carrying it and presume ourselves as the doers. We believe everything that happens in this life journey—profit & loss, difficulties & pleasures, joy & sorrow as ours and think we are the reason for them. We feel that we are the doers and the solution. We claim the outcome.

With the ego called 'I, mine', we turn our life miserable. We mourn as if life is sadness and a stream of tears. Here's a small story.

One day, a man comes crying to Mullah Nasiruddin. Holding the pillar tightly in Nasiruddin's house, the man started venting out his problems, weeping. And said - 'Mullah ji! This pillar is not leaving me just like my problems.'

Then, the Mullah came near the man and asked him to leave the pillar. Now, the pillar is not between the man's hands. He then understood what the Mullah implied - 'Problems didn't hold me. I am holding onto them'. Saying so, he left them and jumped ecstatically.

What is life? What do I do in one year? What do I do in ten years? What will I become in twenty years?

> “Mathematically calculating and churning hours and days is not what life is. It is not at all a predetermined static process. It is not a lifeless rock.”

Life is like a burbling stream flowing from the mountain cliffs effortlessly. It is a consciousness. It is an unimaginable wonder. It is the present that is not a slave to the future. That is why I said that life is 'to live only'.

The beauty of life lies in its mystery.

A magician shows many impossible things. We become enthusiastic to see more of these. Our eyes are fastened by wonder and surprise. We think he is performing some magic. We also believe he has some trick, and we are desperate to know it. However, if we know that trick, we lose its thrill and fun. Won't we? The same thing applies to life as well.

Completely submerging in our jobs is not life. Everything is a business from morning till night - talking, writing, laughing, or crying.

For some, business is life, and for others, life is business. Occupation is a livelihood. We may or may not like the occupation we choose for earning. There is competitiveness in occupation. There is the expectation of outcome. This doesn't mean that we should not pursue any occupation or business. Life is to live beyond all these competitions and expectations. There is completeness in living like this. There is union in living like this.

There will be friction when the goals and means differ. We choose the occupation which yields better earnings. We don't bother about life in the pursuit of earning. That is why there won't be harmony in our life. When there is a gap between living and occupation, we lead a double life. We are being tutored and trained for the professions. Where does life stand in this training?

We are spending 90% of our lives on our occupation.

We are unable to spare time to listen to our inner responses. That is how happiness slowly moves away from our lives. And such a suppressed happiness lies beneath the layers of our hearts. We make many permutations and combinations for a comfortable life. Thereby we make our life complex. We complicate our minds. This leads to conflict, anxiety, disappointment, anger, and jealousy. Let us make life as simple as a stream.

Let us bring it near to our conscience. Let us merge it into the present. However small a mirror is, it shows our reflection. Isn't it? Similarly, however small our life is, there is completeness. It removes the gap between desire and capability. It dissolves the misty cover between life and happiness.

There are six obstacles to happiness.

1. Concentration on others

Other's works, possessions, spending and wealth, attract us. We try to compete with them to make more wealth. Whether in name or fame, wealth or status, we work hard to supersede what others have. As a result, we are unhappy despite achieving many things.

2. The expectation on the future

Creating wealth for the next generations, thirst for overnight fame and living for something else is the main obstacle to our happiness. It makes us sleepless.

3. Becoming a slave to the past

Past incidents, experiences, influences of the dead, and socio-economic situations dictate and discipline us. As a result, instead of living in the present, we are in the effects of the past most of the time, which makes us unhappy.

4. Attachment to faiths and ideologies

We lose ourselves in participating in others' arguments and ideologies. We sacrifice our prudence for some arguments, ideologies and faiths.

5. Reactive lifestyle

90% of our actions are reactive to what's happening around us in our daily lives. Be it a reaction to someone's talk, response to situations, or work - everywhere we observe a reactive lifestyle. We try to derive happiness from things like cars, bungalows, and electronic gadgets as if it is an undertaking. In no time, we lose the joy of buying a new car. In the same way, we derive happiness from others' praises and appreciations. The moment the other person criticizes us, our joy disappears. Remember, happiness dependent upon things and others' opinions is not happiness at all.

6. The ego of 'I, My, Mine'

As mentioned above, the feeling of - 'I am everything, the arrogance that no one should be above me, the selfishness that I need to have everything,' drains happiness.

Where is happiness?

It is within us. You won't find it if you search it elsewhere. The more you explore elsewhere, the farther it gets away. We need to turn our attention from the outside to the inside. We need to touch the depths of happiness inside. Only then can life be filled with joy.

Our happiness is in our hands. It is not dependent on external situations or things. For an infant, the world is delightful. There are no limits to its joy. There are no expectations for its happiness. As we grow older, we are growing nearer to ego and farther from joy.

When we remove all the layers of conditioning, we find our soul. That soul is an entity of happiness, like a baby's smile. The soul refuses all limits. It constantly affirms in man an optimism, never pessimism.

For life, being alive itself is happiness. That happiness has no conditions, expectations or boundaries. That is why we need to treat ourselves as forms of joy. We have to face every situation as part of a joyful game. We need to meet people as they are all players in this game.

The beginning and end of our thoughts should be happiness. They should continue in happiness alone. In every word we speak, in every step we walk, it should be filled with joy. That happiness should not be an enforced one. It is not reactive. Our existence itself is happiness. However small or big our work might be, we should do it with happiness. As small as an act of drinking water also should be done joyfully.

If we want to be happy in all places, at all times, in all things, then we need contentment. Where there is contentment, there is happiness. Where there is an expectation, there is discontentment. Where there is discontentment, desires put us on fire. In that fire, desire turns into the coal of greed. In greed, happiness becomes a mirage.

It is challenging to suppress desires. Even if we do, it won't bring contentment. We can harness desires when we are aware of feelings 'I, my, mine'. As a result, contentment will blossom in everything. Then, instead of searching for happiness in things, situations, and other people, we shall experience pleasure within. We turn into happiness. Happiness becomes our existence and life.

We should live like aquatic creatures in
the ocean of life, not as swimmers.

❑

Success and Failure

'When you carry my dead body across the streets, make sure that both my hands are hanging out to make them visible to everyone.'

You must be wondering who made this strange request. It is said by none other than the world-famous Alexander, The Great.

He answered his baffled followers, saying, 'People need to know that I died with empty hands. Everyone should see my empty hands. Looking at them, they shouldn't try to become

Alexander. I achieved a lot. Yet, there is so much to achieve. My Kingdom is vast. Yet, I am poor.'

Although we all understood what Alexander said, we still want to become as successful as him. Don't we?

Who doesn't want victory? In studies, jobs, arts, sports, music....so on and so forth, we want success in everything. People are after victory. One is treated like a King if one wins or is treated as a pauper. This thought haunts us.

If you want victory, you need capacity. To acquire capacity, you need skill. Skill is attained through practice. Blind practice turns a man mechanical as there is no freedom in it. But creativity and mindful practice go together. Only then can one get the necessary capability.

Society expects subordination, and it is possible only through a mechanical life. That is why society binds a human in the framework of success and failure. It measures everyone with the tape of success and failure. The focus is always on the outcome. Coronation happens only to those who achieve success.

A man cannot produce output as much as a machine does. The required output may be attained when a man works like a machine. He may gain the skill too. But, won't this process crush a man's inner beauty?

Thankfully, the same individual can live happy if he lives with awareness.

What is Success?

It's the point where effort meets desire.

What's Desire?

It's the wish to move from having to becoming.

The mind is the centre for success and failure, not the playground. Yet, we search for the playground and leave the mind behind. We get influenced by the playground. Positions, designations, names, and fame influence a person's heart. Expectations and desires make our ideals run around. When there is ambition, only self-development is visible. As a result, jealousy, hatred, and conflicts arise in our relationships. We desire — political power and leadership, accumulation of wealth, and reputation. If not, we want to become notable spiritual gurus. In all these desires, there's cutthroat competition.

Desire drives a man. This in turn encourages action. Action has the expectation of the outcome and is also inclined towards success. When we meet this expectation, it sows the seed of ego. Failure brings frustration for one who is drowned in the ego of success. Such a heart gets shattered even on minor storms in life.

In that case, can there be an action without expectation of the outcome?

Success and failures are the fuel for one's thoughts. One should not lose life in the snakes and ladder game of success and failure.

What is essential to life?

Of course, every man wishes to live an exciting life. However, that should not be temporary happiness dependent upon success. It should also not be misery that stoops to failure.

The mode of measurement for success and failure are comparisons and competitions. We decide on our plight after comparing it with others. The moment we start comparing, we start competing too. These lead to jealousy, hatred, and revenge. We feel jealous of the wealthy, the influential, who gets good marks, and the famous. These feelings aggravate along with time.

> *How many times have we not failed in our hearts in our race to reach the number one position? Where is the scope for happiness in a leisure less yearning?*

Yes. We are running after someone. We are following. We are complying. We are searching around for our life.

Let's say our neighbour achieved a gold medal in sports. As a result, he got his name and fame. Similarly, a girl we know of got the first rank in All India Institute of Medical Sciences. Another one got a seat along with a scholarship at Massachusetts Institute. In this way, we find many such examples around our vicinity. These examples instigate us to follow them.

Children's successes and failures have become the symbols of parents' prestige.

That is why, more than the children, the parents feel nervous about their children's success. Hence, they cannot see or bear with their failures. Parents are not letting children do anything by themselves. In fact, failure or loss has become a prohibited word in society. Society discriminates and demeans all those who fail.

What is a failure?

When the effort gives way to despair, and pessimism it is termed as failure.

Only when an individual does work without expectations can he attain mastery over anything, says the Bhagavad Gita. It won't happen without performing any action. That is why, unless an individual performs activities without expectations of the outcome, he cannot attain liberation from work. In this journey, he cannot even escape from work.

In the Gita, Sri Krishna advises Arjuna.

karmaṇy-evādhikāras te mā phaleṣhu kadāchana |
mā karma-phala-hetur bhūr mā te saṅgo 'stvakarmaṇi || 2.47 ||

कर्मण्येवाधिकारस्ते मा फलेषु कदाचन ।
मा कर्मफलहेतुर्भूर्मा ते सङ्गोऽस्त्वकर्मणि || 2.47 ||

'You have a right to perform your prescribed duties, but you are not entitled to the fruits of your actions. Therefore, never consider yourself to be the cause of the results of your activities, nor be attached to inaction.'

In this way, one should work as a mere observer and not a doer. Doing so, one will gain mastery over one's work, and as a result, the outcome will come by itself. In anything that one does, physically, mentally and spiritually, one should not have a sense of doership. Therefore, we will be able to focus better on our work than being influenced or disturbed by the anxiety created by the outcome.

Here, not expecting the result doesn't mean one should reject the result. It simply means that we should not be disturbed by the outcome, success or failure. In other words, our happiness should not be a slave to the outcome. So, we should perform our actions naturally but not for success or failure.

In Gandhiji's words,

"Satisfaction lies in the effort, not attainment. Full effort is full victory."

However, if we focus on the outcome, we try to achieve it by whatever means. We sacrifice the means or norms for the end. We defend that if the result is good, one need not worry about the path. We don't hesitate to choose any direction to win competitions or elections. We give importance to power, not to the character. Relationships are giving way to pleasures and convenience. We focus on the accumulation of wealth rather than how we gain it. We are changing work-life happiness to a life of pleasures in this fashion.

We should love our hard work. We should put in the best of our efforts with love. Living through work is happiness in work-life. That is real love for life. Lazily gossiping for some pastime might seem like a pleasure to most. However, a laggard is a slave to the four walls of his house and a burden to himself.

Life is sorrowful for them. The effort is the only way to get out of this darkness.

The sweat that spills in the sincere effort can change one's destiny. The knowledge or wealth that one gains without effort makes a man lazy. Similarly, a loveless work is like a Sun in an eclipse.

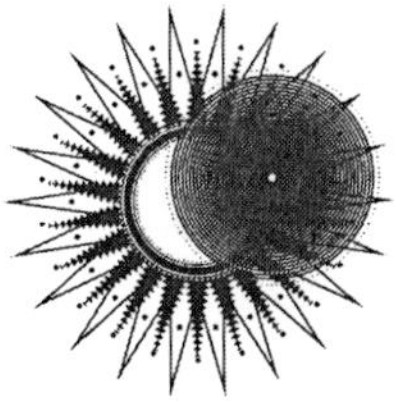

So, what is it to work with love?

Khalil Gibran says,

"*It is to weave the cloth with threads drawn from your heart,*
even as if your beloved were to wear that cloth.

It is to build a house with affection,
even as if your beloved were to dwell in that house.

It is to sow seeds with tenderness and reap the harvest with joy,
even as if your beloved were to eat the fruit.

It is to charge all things you fashion with a breath of your own spirit,
Work is love made visible."

Our society labelled the nature of works as noble or mean, good or bad. Some people are considered superior to others based on their jobs. Similarly, there is a feeling that the literate is superior to the illiterate and white-collared guys are superior to artisans. These have only created differences in the lives of people. People are respected accordingly.

For instance, we respect the businessman who lives on commission more than the farmer who produces the food for everyone.

Today, we are educating our children based on the market. Our education is acutely dependent upon packages and designations. Although packages and designations can build wealth and influence, they cannot transmit light or knowledge.

We think that there should be a goal to live, and in achieving that alone, life has a meaning. For some, the goal is to attain wealth, and for some, it is power. For some, it is fame. Everybody is putting much hard work into achieving their targets. However, we are sacrificing happiness for these short-term gains. As a result, constant conflict, vengeance, and endless expectations give us no respite. We are on the constant lookout for something or the other. In such a condition, how can we live without being selfish?

When we desire something, the fear of not getting it haunts us. That fear is what turns our minds ugly. In fear, we tend to imitate or follow someone.

As a result, we go low on creative abilities and lose our natural self. We will stay poor as long as we expect success, wealth, name, fame, position, and power. Although we display an excellent picture to the external world, we live in constant fear. That kind of fear is what makes our doings very ugly. As a result, life becomes insanely stressful.

Many live their lives melancholically with the thought that they haven't achieved anything significant or haven't reached their destination. They blame everybody around them for their unhappy lives but will never accept responsibility for their wrongdoings. Such negative mindsets find relief in playing the blame game when they face failures.

So, what is essential in life?

To live is essential. We need to know our hearts. We need to look into our inner selves. We need to observe our inner thoughts as-is without alterations. Only when we self-learn who we are do all the required life energies come into existence.

Love Your Path

We can love the work we do only when we love our path.

If our approach is noble, the outcome will naturally be noble.

If we fill our efforts with love, results will come independently.

If we speak gently and precisely, it will bring many hearts together. Or else, the same tongue can distance many.

See the Time As Your Servant

There are many times when we wished that a day should have more than 24 hours. That's because we haven't learnt how to manage time.

We can't fill our stomachs with daydreaming. We have to travel with our tasks along with time. Procrastination breeds laziness.

Let us prioritize the work of the day. These priorities should be born from our hearts. Let us bring them into beautiful masterpieces. Let us walk every day on the shining path of our hearts. There will be no clouds of doubts and fears. Remove the thorns enroute and move on.

Allot the first fifteen minutes of every day to plan the tasks for the day and the last fifteen minutes to evaluate. That is how we gain control over our time.

Befriend Situations and Circumstances

For a minute, let us keep the idea of luck aside. Let us start each day believing that everyone is good and that every situation happens for our good. Let us stop complaining about the unfavourable. Let us befriend ourselves and our path.

Be Aware of Your Heart

Our heart is like an ocean. As we go deep, we understand better. We can see its beats. Many people can't see even its surface correctly. Some smartly dive into and find their inner voice.

Life will, of course, be in constant turmoil with the mind in one place and the heart somewhere else. Once we know our inner voice, the journey will be smooth. Not just that, even our capacity will be utilized entirely, and life energies will be conserved.

There's Nothing Which Can't Be Achieved With Hard Work

We need the effort to get things done. There are no alternatives or shortcuts. This effort should not be mechanical. It should give happiness and fill enthusiasm in us every day. We should enjoy working.

Notice that nothing comes to us on its own. We should work to our capacity and abilities while correcting our mistakes.

Behind Every Success, There is Failure

If we run away from failure, we are the primary reason for the failure to win. We should recognize that we are not working for either success or failure. Let us have our heart only on the path. Whatever be the outcome, let us accept it gracefully.

When we look into the histories of great people, we will notice that they maintained equanimity in both successes and failures. For example, Abraham Lincoln became the President of America despite many shortcomings. That is why let us accept failures just as we accept successes. In that way, there won't be any scope for dejection.

Thomas Alva Edison failed at least 10,000 times in inventing the light bulb.

In 1914, the laboratory he built got destroyed in a fire accident. Edison said, 'There is a great value even in destruction. Thank Cod, all our mistakes got burnt and turned into ashes. With Cod's grace, we can start fresh' without feeling anxious.

Success and failure are not related to life but to life events. Both success and failure are not permanent things in life. They are like tides in the ocean. Highs and lows keep moving and interchanging.

Success and failure are inseparable. There will be a conflict if you accept one and reject the other. It is like embracing the day and rejecting the night. Life will be remarkable only if we accept both without choosing one. Hence, accept both without pride and prejudice. Learn from them and progress forward.

❑

The Oceans within Us

There is a tree even in a man and a sky above that tree. In that sky, there are clouds, and they give rain. So, a flow is born of that rain which turns into a pond, a river, a sea, and a mighty ocean.

A man's childhood still plays with the shells on that seashore.

The youth still make adventurous journeys on that ocean.

With frayed eyes, old age watches the truth of life found in the interiors of the abyss.

All such inner oceans show us the way out from the inside to play the game of life.

❑